Mended Pieces

T. Brown - Champion

This is a work of fiction. Any references or similarities to actual events, real people, dead, or living, or to real locals are intended to give this book a sense of reality. Any similarity in the characters, places, names, and incidents is entirely coincidental.

Copyright © 2010 T. Brown-Champion

All rights reserved. No part of this book may be reproduced in any form or by any means without prior consent of the Publisher.

ISBN-13: 978-1461034643
ISBN-10: 1461034647

Website: www.mendedpieces.org
Email Address: tbrownchampion@gmx.com

Dedication

I would like to, first and foremost, dedicate this book to God. If it wasn't for giving me the words and the knowledge, I would not have known that I had the ability to write. I thank you so much for blessing me. You have always told me that an idle mind is the devil's workshop. So I thank you for changing my heart and my mind.

Amen

I am also dedicating this book to my dearly beloved late grandmother, Sallie Mae Woods-Brown. Grandmother, words cannot express the love and devotion that you have given to your children and your grandchildren. With the help of God, you have raised nine amazing children. Thank you for being the light of the Brown family. You may be gone but your light is still shining. I love you and I miss you, Grandma.

"I can do all things through God who strengthens me."
Philippians 4:13

To Bobbie

Thank you for your
Support

Bruce Champion

Table of Content

My loving family	3
The hospital visit	7
A new beginning	11
The love of my life	15
Prom	19
A scary moment	25
My best friend Jessica	39
Catherine	43
Christmas	47
The wedding	53
Twins	59
Trying to make ends meet	63
Seeking my mother's advice	71
My yearly doctor's examination	75
A visit from an old friend	89
Our precious gift	97
Anniversary trip	99
Deon's new attitude	109
The doctor visit	115
An outrageous conversation	125
Kimberly	129
Changes	135
My first job	139
Kimberly speaks out	141
Kimberly's party	145
Full of anger	149
Kimberly tells all	153
In the midst of my storm	157
Keeping secrets	161
My heart can't take anymore	167
The move	177
Praying for Deon	185
Mended pieces	197

Acknowledgments

To my gifts from God, Tim and my children, I thank you for your love and support, and also allowing yourselves to love God before anything else.

"The steps of a good man are ordered by the Lord,
he delighteth in his way."
Psalms 37:23

"Lo, children are an heritage of the Lord:
and the fruit of the womb is his reward."
Psalms 127:3

To my amazing parents, I am so grateful for the parents that I have been blessed with. They equipped me with the values and morals to be the daughter, sister and parent that I am today. I love you both so very much.

To my entire family, friends, church family, my editors and my Sisters of Divine Women of Strength, thank you for taking this journey with me. I love you all.

Mended Pieces

My loving family

The year I turned twelve, life as I knew it was about to be changed forever. I was in the seventh grade and my brother, Robert, Jr., was just two years older than me. My parents, Karen and Robert Sanders, Sr. had been married for 14 years. I've always said that whenever I get older, I want my marriage to be just like my parents'. They never fought, and always showed us lots of love. My father always made sure that he worked, so that my mother could stay home and take care of us. Whenever my father got paid, he always gave his paycheck to my mother. He knew that she was better with money than he was, therefore he wanted her to make sure that the bills were paid, and that there were groceries for the family. I am Melissa Sanders and this is the story of my life.

I remember clearly the last normal Sunday dinner my family and I shared together. We held hands and prayed. We always prayed before each meal and my mother encouraged us to pray without ceasing. I made sure I told my mother and my father that I loved them. The next morning, my father had to go to work at six o'clock. Normally, he goes in at seven o'clock. But on this one particular day, he had to leave a little early. Before he left to go to work, we were already awake. My mom had gotten up early to cook us all a hot breakfast before we started our day. After my father had finished eating his breakfast, he gave me a huge hug and kiss, and told me to make sure that I did well in school. I always got a hug and a kiss from my dad, but this time it felt a little different. He gave my brother a hug and told Robert, Jr. to make sure that he took care of the family while he was at work. My mother looked at my dad and told him he didn't have to worry because Robert Jr. usually does a great job.

As my father was heading to the door to leave for work, he looked at all of us and said that he loved us, and as soon as he got off, he would hurry home. We knew we were our father's top priority, because he always showed us love. Spending quality time with his family was more important to him than anything else in the world. I was kind of sad to see my dad leave that morning, but at the same time, I was happy because I knew that he was coming back home. I told my father that when he gets off, we will have his favorite dinner cooked for him, which is steak and potatoes.

"Steak and potatoes," my dad replied. "Melissa, I can hardly wait."

With a smile, my mother told my dad that she loved him very much, and to make sure that he drove safely. He told her that he would. I thought that was very special because every morning my mom and dad would give each other a kiss before leaving for work. As my mom closed the door behind my dad, she went into the kitchen to wash the dishes. She told my brother and I to go ahead and get ready for school. About fifteen minutes later, the telephone rang. This was a little unusual, because no one calls this early in the morning. As my mom answered the phone, she realized that it was my father on the other end. He had pulled over to the local convenience store to use the payphone.

"Hey honey, I was just calling to let you know that it's foggy and raining outside, so please drive safely when you take the kids to school."

My mother replied, "I will, and thanks for the call."
Thirty minutes later, as we were leaving for school, my mother yelled, "Your father called and said it's raining, so make sure you get your umbrellas."

We were about to walk out of the house, when all of a sudden, someone knocked at the door. My mom looked through the peep hole, and saw two police officers. She looked at us, and then asked if we were playing on the telephone, calling 911. We told her, "No, ma'am."

As she opened the door, the officers asked my mother for her last name. "Sanders," she replied.

"Are you married to Robert Sanders?" the officer asked.

"Yes, why do you ask?" my mother replied.

"Well, we would like to know if it's okay to come in, out of the rain." My mom hesitated because she was hoping that my dad wasn't in any trouble.

"Is everything okay?" my mother asked.

"Ma'am, we would rather come in and speak to you."

The officers entered the house. Deeply concerned, Robert, Jr. and I stood behind my mom.

One officer said, "Please have a seat, ma'am."

As my mom took her seat, she had seen a tear forming out of one of the officers eyes.

Once again she asked them, "Is everything okay?"

"We are sorry to inform you that your husband has been involved in a terrible car accident. He had to be rushed to the hospital," the officer stated.

I could not believe what I had just heard.

The officer went on to say, "I'm sorry to say, but he's in critical condition."

My mom's head went back and hit the pillow on the sofa. She sat up and replied emphatically, "There is no way that you can be talking about my husband, because I just got off the phone with him!"

Both officers sat with blank expressions on their faces.

"Are you sure it is him?"

"Yes, ma'am, we're sure."

They showed my mom some papers that were in his car, along with his driver's license. My brother and I started hugging each other, and began to cry. My mom knew at that point that it was my dad.

"How did this happen?" she asked.

"Well, ma'am, there was a semi-truck broken down, and a portion of the trailer was blocking the highway."

The foul weather did not allow my father to see everything that was in front of him on the road.

One of the officers said, "Mrs. Sanders, by the time your husband realized that he was too close to the truck, it was too late, and he collided with it."

I could barely stand to hear anymore. I felt as if my heart was being ripped to pieces.

The officer continued, "Your husband began spinning in the middle of the road, hit the median, and flipped over. The truck driver was okay, but your husband was not. He was non-responsive. That's when we knew that he had to be air-lifted to the nearest hospital."

The pain and hurt that was in my mother's face is something that I will never forget. There was a silence for about three minutes, and then the officer began to say, "I am so sorry, but I think the best thing for you and your kids to do is to go and be by his side."

The Hospital Visit

My mother quickly grabbed her keys and purse, and we rushed to the hospital. When we arrived, we had to wait because my father was in surgery. The hospital staff had led us into a quiet little room that they called the chapel. As we entered the room, the lights were dim but my eyes were drawn to the picture of Jesus in the garden of Gethsemane. In the picture, Jesus bowed down in prayer, and was sweating great drops of blood. I felt at that moment that He too was praying for my father.

I saw my mom reach into her purse, and take out her Bible. She started declaring life over my father, reading scripture after scripture out loud. Then she began to weep. My mother cried out to God, piercing my heart with each cry. Now the woman I always looked to for my own strength was a basket case. She repeatedly mumbled those words that the officers told her, "Critical condition."

At that moment, I felt the touch of my brother's hand on my shoulder. He pulled me close to him and we prayed together. His prayers assured me that everything was going to be okay. But something inside me knew that this just did not feel right.

The doctors had been operating on him for hours, it seemed. I could not believe that it was God's will for my father's life to end in such tragedy. The devil is a liar!

After many hours of weeping and praying, we were all exhausted. Yet somehow, in the midst of all this, there was a peace I could not understand. The Peace of God began to fill that little chapel room in the hospital and my mother's sobbing began to soften. I felt, deep down inside, my mother knew that our father wasn't coming home.

I didn't want to accept that, because all I could think about was the last words that I said to him, which was that I was going to cook his favorite meal when he got home. My dad promised me he was coming home! So I knew that when my dad makes me a promise, he would always keep it.

All of a sudden, the doors opened, and the doctor came into the chapel. He asked us all to come into his office. The expression on his face didn't indicate anything positive. The doctor began to speak, saying, "The accident that your husband was involved in was a very bad one. We have done all that we could do. His impact with the median, combined with flips, was more than enough to cause him to be brain dead."

My mom yelled so loud, "No! Don't tell me that!" The doctor told my mom that our father didn't make it. He had tried his best to hold on, but he couldn't. My mom went numb for a while, and she wouldn't say a word. My brother and I just stood there in shock because we knew our lives were never going to be the same again. I never thought this morning, when I kissed my dad and told him that I loved him, it would have been my last time seeing him. In the back of my mind, I felt that my dad knew he wouldn't be coming home that day.

The death of my father really placed a scar on my life. I knew that it was going to be a very difficult time for my mom, because she had always said she couldn't live without my dad. Besides us, he was all that she had. I was crying so hard that I was losing my breath. I still felt the kiss on my face from my daddy. His scent was still on my clothes and I smelled his cologne as if he was right in the room with us.

The doctor asked Mama if she wanted to go and say her final farewell to my father. Mama looked at the doctor with anger in her eyes. She asked him if he was sure that they had done all they could do. He told her that they had done just that, and even went beyond to try to save him. "When he came in, he was already brain dead," said the doctor.

With a rage that I had never seen in her before, Mama began to scream at the doctor. She began to beat on the wall with her fists clenched tight. "He's all I have… no, no, no… please tell me this is not happening! Lord, how am I going to make it without Robert?" My mother's emotions came in waves, first sadness, then anger, and then more sadness. This moment seemed like it lasted forever. Would she ever be able to accept that my father was gone? Would I?

Mama decided to calm down, and go say her farewell. My brother and I couldn't do it just yet. We just wanted to remember him the way he left us back home. I didn't want to believe that he was gone. I never thought that at my age, I would be fatherless.

As Mama went into the room, my brother and I stood on the outside of the door in the hallway. She was talking to my dad, telling him that she loved him, and she will do whatever it takes to be strong for my brother and me. While she was talking to my father, she began to cry. All of a sudden, she stopped talking. I decided to look in and check on her. She had her head across my father's chest. I really didn't know what my mother was thinking. Knowing her, she was trying to see if she could hear a heartbeat. I knew she just could not accept that he was gone.

For about a week, my brother and I had to cook dinner and ride the bus to school because our mom would not leave her room. She stayed in there until it was time for my dad's funeral. At first, she wasn't going to have one because she didn't want to sit there, looking at my dad motionless in a casket. However, she knew it wouldn't be fair for his friends not to be able to express their final condolences.

My brother and I were glad when the funeral and burial were finally over. We just needed our time to mourn the loss of our father. At the funeral, the pastor read from the book of Matthew chapter five, "Blessed are they that mourn: for they shall be comforted." I knew that promise from God's Word was the only reason I was feeling any kind of comfort. Even still, I knew that I would never feel completely whole because I was a daddy's girl. Without him,

I was broken. I really didn't think that my mom could find the strength to make it without my dad.

A new beginning

It took my mother about two months just to get her life back on track because she knew that she had two children to care for. I think the hardest thing about my father's death was the fact that it was unexpected, and his life insurance policy was only enough to cover his funeral expenses. My mom was trying to sue the trucking company, but they were giving her the run-around. So in the meantime, my mom had to work two jobs, and also get government assistance.

That was the hardest thing for my mom, because working was something that she had never done. She always depended on my father for everything. My brother and I were so ashamed because we never had to live that way. Going to the grocery store with paper money, with different pictures on it, was so embarrassing. Whenever we saw someone that we knew, we waited until they had left the grocery store before buying our food. We refused to let anyone know that we were on food stamps. Our mom told us that we shouldn't act that way, because we should be thankful that we had other means of help. She told me that I would be surprised how many kids at my school were on food stamps, or any kind of government assistance. My mom may have been right, but I knew how the kids were at my school. They would make fun of you and tell other kids your business. Not me! I refused to let anyone find out. I always told myself that whenever I have kids, they would never have to worry about government assistance. I felt like the two jobs that my mom was working would have covered us for food, and whatever else that we needed. Well, I guess I was wrong.

Two years later, my mom finally got the phone call that we had been waiting for. It was the court system. They told her they needed her to come down to the courthouse the next day. My mom had a feeling what it was about, but she just wouldn't say a word.

The next day came; my mom, my brother and I were at the court house as soon as the doors were opened. The clerk called her into the room but she was not alone. The owner of the trucking company that killed my dad was also there. My mom's hands began to shake and she had a tear inside her eye. As she took her seat, the owner offered my mom a settlement check of $100,000. My mom looked at us, and she was speechless. I wanted so badly to hit my mom just to make sure that she heard him right. When my mom finally spoke, she wanted it to be known that this money would never bring her husband back and she told them about the fact that she had to work two jobs to provide for us. While I was listening, I just wanted my mom to say, "Yes, I will take the check," but she continued talking. I think my mom had so much to get off her chest, that after she was done talking, he tore the check up and apologized for what had happened to our dad.

The judge was in tears after my mom finished saying all she had to say. He told her that there was no way that he would let her leave this court room with only a check for $100,000. He said that she shouldn't have had to wait as long as she did for the money. He wanted to know if she could come up with all her check stubs from her second job over the past two years. He also asked for proof of any child-care expenses for anyone who had to watch us while she was working. My mom looked at the judge and told him that it would take hours before she would be able to come up with anything like that.

He told her, "Don't worry. I will allow you to get your figures together." The expression on my mother's face was one of thankfulness.

The judge continued to say, "Mrs. Sanders, it has been way too long for you not to have your money. I am here to apologize on behalf of the trucking company and the court system. I want you to know that we have failed, and I will be the first to make sure this will never happen to you or anyone else again."

While my mom was writing down the figures, I couldn't believe how much she came up with, and it was looking very good to me. The amount totaled a sum of $250,000. My brother and I were in the corner smiling at each other whispering, "We are going to be rich!" The only thing we could think of was that we were going to be off of food stamps!

Once the judge looked over my mom's figures, he came up with his own settlement, which was so much more than the original settlement! He offered my mom a settlement for $500,000 for pain and distress. He also awarded her another $500,000 for having to work two jobs, and for having to find someone to keep us. Those two settlements by the judge would make us millionaires!

"No parent should have to be away from their children all day," the judge said.

He continued, "Do you feel as if my ruling is fair, Mrs. Sanders?"

My mother thanked the judge and said, "I never thought for one moment that my family and I would ever receive a settlement this large."

The owner of the trucking company was trying to fight the settlement, but the judge told him there was no way he would allow that to happen. He told him that he would have two months to give my mother the settlement.

My brother and I looked at my mom with our eyes bulging out of our heads. At that moment, we were the happiest kids on the planet! We didn't have to worry about food stamps or public assistance ever again!

The love of my life

Two years later, my brother Robert Jr. was in his first year of college. I was in the eleventh grade and I met a cute guy named Deon. Being a junior in high school was perfect; my mother had finally allowed me to start dating. With his good looks and intelligence, Deon was well known and well liked around school. He was also the quarterback of our football team. I had a crush on him since last year. But I knew my mom meant business when she told me that I could not date anyone.

One day, Deon approached me and said that I was a very beautiful girl. He also said, "If you are this beautiful, then I would love to see your mother."

Smiling from ear to ear, I replied, "That's a good one." I felt as if he was very respectful.

He asked me, "What is your name and do you have a boyfriend?"

"Melissa," I replied.

"That's a very beautiful name."

I was very surprised because he could have had anyone in the school but he chose me. I hesitated for a minute, but I answered quickly and said, "No, I don't have a boyfriend."

"Well, I just wanted to tell you that I have had my eye on you for the past year, and I've been waiting for the right time to approach you."

Deon felt as if I wasn't interested. I was laughing while he was talking to me. He stopped talking just to ask me what was so funny. I told Deon that I had a crush on him for the past year as well. The only hold-up was that my mom told me that I could not date anyone until I was in the eleventh grade.

I told him, "As bad as I wanted to talk to you, I had to make sure

I respected my mother's wishes."

"I totally understand," he said.

He wanted me to know that I was worth waiting for. And if I didn't mind, he would like to be my boyfriend. My heart started tingling because Deon had been the man of my dreams for the past year.

I didn't know how to act because the time finally came for me to start dating. I told Deon that we could take it one step at a time, but I made sure he knew that I was feeling him. I guess my "one day at a time" speech did not have any bearing because we started dating immediately.

The best part about being with Deon is that we were both virgins. I was really surprised to learn that a guy as cute as Deon was still a virgin. I still didn't know how to kiss. The only man that I ever kissed was my daddy; therefore, it's been a while.

A week later, I decided to take Deon home to meet my mom. She told me that before I got serious about dating anyone, she wanted to meet the person. I was very nervous about my mother meeting him. She's the type of woman who will tell you the truth about someone. She appeared to like him, so I was happy. Whenever she would ask him a question, he would answer it with a "yes, ma'am" or a "no, ma'am." Mama told him that she likes a respectful young man for her daughter.

While she was talking to Deon, I was giving her the eye. I wanted her to know that I didn't want her to embarrass me. My mother must have done a great job because Deon came over on a regular basis after that.

I knew our relationship was good, because a week later, he took me to meet his mother. She was a very nice person. I was so happy that she treated me nicely. I was really hoping that I would get the chance to meet his father also.

"Deon, will I ever get the chance to meet your father?" I asked.

"No, Melissa, not at this time."

"Well, will it be in the near future?"

"Probably not any time soon, because he is in jail."

"I'm sorry to hear that, Deon."

"It's alright; it's not your fault."

"I know that it is not any of my business, but is he okay?"

"Oh yes, Melissa, he is just fine. Seven years ago, my mother and I had to put my father in jail. Ever since I was a little boy, my dad would put his hands on my mom; he cheated, and he was also an alcoholic."

"Wow, I can only imagine how you felt," I replied with a disturbed look on my face.

Deon continued, "I would get very upset. I begged him to take his hands off my mom 'or else'. He looked at me with his evil eyes and said, 'Or else what?' I was nervous because I didn't know what else to say. I was very over-protective of my mom. He grabbed me by my arm. Then he pushed me out of the room and shut the door."

"Oh my goodness, Deon, I cannot believe what I am hearing."

"I tried my best to get back into the room to save my mom, but he had the door locked. I knocked and kicked very hard on the door, but he still wouldn't open it. I knew right then and there, if I didn't try to save my mom, he might have killed her. The only thing that I could think of was to call the police.
Once they got there, they kicked down the bedroom door. They found my dad on top of my mom while she was knocked out cold. She was unconscious until the next day when she opened her eyes inside the hospital room. That was the scariest moment of my life!"

"Wow, Deon, do you ever regret calling the police on your dad?"

"Melissa, I do not regret it at all because I was trying to make sure that my mother was safe. I felt as if that was my job. I believe that if a man doesn't take care of his mother, then he won't take care of his wife."

"Deon, that is so true. I will always remember that. I can tell that you are a special person, and I love you for that."

"I love you too, Melissa."

Our relationship had become so strong that we were still dating our senior year in high school. I was still happy to know that Deon never asked me for sex, but I must admit, we did kiss and it got so intense that we had to stop. I became a little scared, because I had a different kind of feeling running through my body. This was a feeling that I had never experienced in my life.

Prom

A month later, Deon asked me if I wanted to go to our Senior Prom. I was excited because this was our last year at our school. I knew it would be a special night for the both of us.

The night of prom, Deon came over to my house and picked me up. My mom took lots of pictures and told me to be safe and that she loved me. As I gave my mom a hug on the way out, I saw tears in her eyes.

"Are you going to be alright, Mom?"

"Yes, I just thought about your father, that's all."

"I know. I thought about him earlier."

"Yes, your father and I always talked about this very moment and I just wish he were here to see his beautiful daughter."

"Me too, Mom, but I know he is up above looking down on me."

"Yes, I know. He always said that when this day came, he was going to be your date!"

With the biggest smile on my face, I told my mother that it would have been an honor to go to prom with my dad.

I gave my mom a kiss and told her that everything was going to be okay. She reminded Deon to drive safely and to take good care of her daughter. She whispered in my ear and told me to make sure that I came home no later than 2:00 am. I was as happy as ever to get a late curfew.

While Deon and I were at prom, all of a sudden, he became bored.

"Do you want to go for a walk on the beach, babe?"

"Sure, just make sure that I make it home no later than 1:45," I replied.

"That shouldn't be a problem, because we still have a couple of hours to spare."

As we walked on the beach, we stopped to look at the water. Deon held my hand and started to kiss me. I tried to back away, because I could remember the last time I kissed him. My hormones had started doing something that I never felt before. He pulled me closer to him and told me that everything was going to be okay. I felt like I could trust him, because we had been together for over a year.

He asked me if I wanted to go and sit in the car. I agreed, because there were too many people out there. There was no telling who knew my mom. As we were sitting in his car, Deon started kissing me and began rubbing my chest. I didn't know what to do, because it was starting to feel good. He began to move my chair back. That's when I knew that this was going to be more than a kiss. He started touching me all over and I asked him to stop. All I could see was my mother's face staring at me. As time went on, her face disappeared.

Deon removed all my clothing and started to do something that was beyond my control. I began to wonder if Deon was really a virgin or not.

"Deon, what are you doing to me?"

"Just relax and lie back, babe."

I felt, deep down inside, that he loved me, so I decided to do just what he said. He reached inside his pocket and pulled out a condom. My eyes were so big that it felt like they were bulging out of my head. I was saying to myself, "My mother is really going to kill me." That was because I realized that my life would never be the same again. I would no longer be a virgin. At that moment, I had to make a choice, but the more Deon kissed me, the more the choice was clear. My body had a mind of its own, it seemed. I wanted to tell him to stop, but the words would not come out. At that point, things had gotten out of control. We were at the point of no return.

As I walked inside my house, my mother was standing there,

waiting for me.

"Did you enjoy yourself?" she asked.

"Yes," I replied as I tried to go into the bathroom.

"Did you two do anything that I would not have wanted you to do?"

At that moment, I froze. Then I replied, "No, ma'am, we just had lots of fun."

"Okay, I was just making sure. So tell me about it! What did you two do?"

"Well, of course, we went to prom; we enjoyed ourselves while we were there…He is a really good dancer."

"Oh really, so he can dance, huh?"

"Yes, indeed."

"Well, that's nice."

"Yeah, I know, after prom, we chatted with our friends, got something to eat, and then he brought me home."

"I'm glad you had a good time."

"Alright, Mama, I'm going to bed now. I am tired."

The next day, I thought I was in the clear, but my mother asked me the same dreaded question, one more time, just for her clarification.

"Melissa, are you sure that you and Deon did not do anything that I would not have been happy about last night?"

"No, ma'am, there was nothing extra. We were just having a good time and really getting to know each other more."

"Okay, I was just asking because I know that you two are both attracted to each other. You are young, and there are many mistakes that can be made by couples that young, especially on prom night."

"I completely understand, Mom."

I could not say anything at the time because I was still in shock by what I just heard from my mother.

"Melissa, I just want you to tell me the truth, because for one thing, it will help me keep my trust in you, and it will help you to get it off your chest."

"Yes, ma'am," I replied. Goodness gracious, she keeps asking me the same thing. She makes me wonder, was she nearby spying on me?

I told my mother everything but the most important thing: I was no longer a virgin. I felt as if she did not need to know that at the time, so I left that part out. I just hoped that she didn't find out. I knew that she would be highly disappointed.

Later that night, as I attempted to go to bed, the only thing I was thinking to myself was, I don't know what I would do if my mom found out about me having sex. I knew, deep down in my heart, she would make me stop talking to Deon. I just had to keep this to myself. I loved Deon so much, and I just could not afford to lose him at this time. The only thing I could think of was to pray. I really needed to ask God for His forgiveness of my sins.

The next morning, my mom was up cooking breakfast before we went to church.

"Good morning, Mom."

"Good morning, baby."

"I am really tired, Mom. Is it alright if I pass on church this morning?"

"There is absolutely no way that I am going to allow that to happen, and don't you ever fix your mouth to ask me a question like that again!"

"Okay, Mom."

"Baby, I just want you to realize that without God, we are nothing. I want you to give Him some of your time today."

"I understand, Mom."

"Okay good, now eat your food and go get ready for church."

"Yes, ma'am."

I am really glad that I was obedient and went to church like my mother said. During church, I felt the presence of the Holy Spirit to the point where I caught the Holy Ghost. After church, it felt as if all of the problems in my life were lifted off my shoulders. I felt "extra" joy within my heart. At this point, I was sure that nothing could go wrong in my life.

Maybe a week or so later, my mother showed more concern about me, saying that she had a dream about fish. I knew what those dreams meant, because when I was a young girl, I would hear my mother and her sister's talk about fish. I never understood the reason, until I put it all together, because each time, there were always someone pregnant. I guess that's what I got for being nosy. This terrified me because it seemed as if she knew for a fact that I had sex.

"What are you talking about, Mom? Since you are talking about fish so much, maybe you should fry some."

"This is not a joking matter, Melissa. I am serious!"

"Okay, Mom."

At that point, I realized that my mother had serious concerns about me.

A scary moment

Exactly one month after prom, one morning I was in the bathroom about to wash before leaving the house. All of a sudden, I began to feel a little dizzy. I didn't know what was wrong with me. Until my stomach began turning and my face was drenched with sweat. I decided not to tell my mother because she would have probably turned into the overprotective mother. She would make sure I was eating my veggies and taking my cough medicine. Speaking of veggies and cough medicine, I remember on that day I had an awful taste in my mouth that I had never tasted before. I began to pray, "Lord, please help me feel better. I just don't know what I should do."

As I sat on the side of the bathtub, I began to vomit. I didn't know if I was coming down with something, or if the eggs that my mom cooked earlier were tainted.

"Are you alright in there, Melissa?" shouted my mother.

"I'm fine, Mom, just feeling a little sick, that's all, but I should be alright."

"Okay, well hurry because we have somewhere to be in a few."

"Yes, ma'am."

My mother gave me a look that I had never seen before when she realized that I was throwing up. As I was getting ready to leave the house, Deon called.

"Hey, what's going on, Melissa?"

"Hi Deon, how are you?"

"I'm fine; I was just calling to see how you were doing."

"Well, I was feeling a little sick to my stomach earlier, but I think I'm alright now."

"Wow, I'm sorry to hear that. Are you sure that you're okay?"

"Yes, I believe so."

"Are you sure, Melissa?"

"Yes! Why do you keep asking me that?"

"Okay, I want you to relax and take a deep breath because I have a confession to make."

When I heard the words "relax" and "take a deep breath", I was immediately startled.

"A confession?" I asked.

"Yes, a confession."

"Okay, well what is it? I don't have long to talk because I have somewhere to go."

"Okay, when we had sex that one time, I realized that I did not have the condom on correctly, and it was an old condom that I found a while ago."

"Oh my goodness!" I could not believe what I just heard. "You mean to tell me that you had sex with me with an expired condom?"

"Yes, baby, I am so sorry, Melissa. At that point, I was only worried about my hormones and didn't think about what the future would bring."

"Well, where did you find the condom?" I asked.

"I found it in my mom's room. She used to have a stash of condoms saved for when she and my father would have sex. She didn't trust him because she suspected that he was sleeping with other women."

"Wow, sleeping with other women?"

"Yes, but I wanted to call to let you know that there is a chance that you could be pregnant."

"What? Did you just say pregnant? The devil is a liar! There is no way that can be true and I am not about to sit here and listen to that nonsense!"

"I know you are upset right now, Melissa, but please take what I am telling you into consideration."

"Whatever! My cycle will be on next week and I will let you know when that happens. I refuse to accept the possibility that I am pregnant. I only have one more month of school then I will be finished."

"I understand everything that you are saying, Melissa, but I am only telling you this now so that there won't be any surprises later."

"But Deon, we are too young for this and we both have promising futures ahead of us."

"I know, Melissa, but it's reality."

"Great! Now my mother is calling me. I will talk to you later."

"Okay bye."

"Bye."

"Yes, Mother?"

"Melissa, let's go and take a ride, so we can talk and get some ice cream."

What is it that my mother has to talk to me about? Well, ice cream does sound great!

"Melissa, I really have a lot on my mind."

"Like what?"

"I do want to believe that you and Deon didn't do anything on prom night, but if you were anything like me, I wouldn't tell the truth either."

"Mother, please tell me what you are getting at."

"Melissa, I can think back when your dad and I went to the prom."

"Mother, you have already told me about this."

"Just listen."

"Yes, ma'am."

"As I was saying, your dad and I were having fun. As it became late, your dad knew that I only had about an hour before he had to take me home. So your dad had the nerve to ask me if I wanted to leave and go walking on the beach. I didn't care because I really wanted to spend as much time as I could with him. Melissa, as we started walking, girl, your daddy became a little frisky."

"Mama!"

"No, Melissa, just listen. Your dad started kissing me on my neck, and began to rub his hands all over my back. I had never experienced anything like that in my life."

"I don't know if I want to sit here and listen to my mother's and father's experience with prom."

"Melissa, are you listening?"

"Yes, Mother."

"Well, until that night, I was a virgin."

"Mama, I don't want to hear this!"

"No, I want you to know about my prom night because that is when I became pregnant with your brother."

"Mama, I don't want to hear anymore."

"Well, you are going to listen. You need to listen. Melissa, I was so scared to tell my mom."

"I bet you were."

"I was really scared to tell my dad."

"Why was that?"

"My father was already working two jobs. They were both busy trying to raise six kids."

"I could understand that."

"And here I was, still in high school and pregnant."

Lord, give me strength. I am so nervous and scared just sitting here and listening to my mother talk about her past life. As I was watching and listening to my mother talk, a tear began to fall out of her eye.

I quickly asked Mother, "Are you okay?"

"I am. I was just thinking."

"I know that was the past, but what are you thinking about?"

"Well, I had a thought that I could have been pregnant, but I thought Robert and I didn't spend enough much time together to conceive."

I thought to myself, "I feel the same way."

"Melissa?"

"Yes."

"I didn't find out until I was about five and a half months

pregnant. The strangest thing about it, I was still having my period."

"Okay, Mama, how did you find out?"

"My mother had taken me to see my doctor, so I could have my yearly checkup. While I was there, they told me that I had gained a lot of weight since the last time I was there. They asked me, was I sexually active?"

"What did you tell them?"

"I looked like I was in shock. I asked them, 'Did you say sexually active?' I responded, 'How in the world could you ask me that?'"

"Well, what did you tell them?"

"I told them that I didn't know anything about having sex."

"Mama, you didn't tell them the truth."

"I realized that after my nurse looked at me."

"How did she look?"

"As if I was full of lies. She asked me if I minded taking a urine test."

"Well, did you?"

"I didn't know what a urine test involved, so I didn't mind. I looked at the nurse and told her it was no problem. I wanted to act as if I was big and bold. Girl, I wanted so badly for my mother to think I was still a virgin.
Before I left the room, I heard the nurse whispering to my mother, saying they would like to administer a pregnancy test."

"Mama, I know your heart dropped."

"Yes, Melissa, it did."

"So what did you say?"

"Nothing, I just left the room."

"Wow, Mama."

"All I could do was pray and call out to God, asking Him, 'Lord, please don't let them do any pregnancy test on me.' I told Him I just couldn't face my mother or my father at a time like this. I knew, growing up, I was always told that prayer changes things, but not this time."

"Mama, I know you were scared."

"Yes, baby, I was because the thought of being pregnant at an early age was terrifying."

I was thinking the same thing to myself. Then I asked, "What did you do next?"

"As I was in the bathroom, I started praying again."

"Mama!"

"Melissa, if you were in this situation, you would understand."

"So now what did your prayer say?"

"I said, 'Lord, please, when I pee in this cup, please let this test come back negative!' I didn't know that I was so close to God until that day. I asked God one more time to please let this test come back negative, because I knew that Robert had worn a condom."

"I know, Mama, because they said condoms always work."

"No, baby, that is not true. I felt the same way. I told God that there was no way that I could be pregnant. Like my girlfriends and I had always thought, condoms were one hundred percent. Well, that was what my friends said."

"So what happened next?"

"After I finished the test, I waited about ten minutes then I went back into the room where my mother and the doctor were. He told me that the nurse would be back in a few minutes."

"Mama, how in the world could you have sat there in front of your mother, while waiting on your results?"

"I really don't know, Melissa. That was the hardest thing for me to do. After five minutes, the nurse entered the room."

"So what did she tell you?"

"She didn't."

"What do you mean?"

"Well, she stepped in only to ask my doctor to step out of the room. Melissa, I glanced at my mom with my hands shaking. My mother looked and asked me again if I had something to tell her before they came back into the room."

"Mama, I don't know what I would have done at that point."

"I did what I knew was best."

"What was that?"

"Well, I took a deep breath and decided to tell my mother the truth."

"You did?"

"Yes, because I felt like I was already busted. I wanted her to know what really happened on the night of my prom."

"Mama, did you tell her the truth?"

"Yes, I did. I told her that Robert and I had sex."

"You did?"

"Yes, I told her that I knew it was wrong, but I didn't think anything would have happened. I also explained to her that he had worn a condom. I wanted my mother to know that Robert and I had made a big mistake. I didn't think I was pregnant because it was our first time. I thought it would take more than one time to get pregnant."

"So what did Grandmother say?"

"My mom told me to stop talking. She wanted me to know that I should never call a pregnancy a mistake. She also told me that she already knew my results. She just wanted me to tell her the truth first. The doctor had read them to her before I entered the room."

"Mother, were you surprised?"

"Yes, Melissa, I was, but I was really surprised when my mother told me that she already had a feeling I was pregnant."

"How was that?"

"She told me that I had a strange look when the doctor had questioned me."

"Hold on, Mama. I don't know if I could have stood there facing my mother, the doctor and the nurse."

"I was so much in shock that I had to ask my mother to repeat what she had just said to me."

"What were you expecting her to say?"

"I wanted to make sure that she just said that I was pregnant. I looked at her with tears rolling down my face. I told her that there was no way that I could be pregnant. I wanted to know, how in the world I could be pregnant? As the doctor and the nurse came back into the room, they told me that it was for the best that my mother and I talked it out before they had given me my results."

"Mother, were you upset with them?"

"Yes a little, but they had apologized for my mom getting the results before I did. But they felt that it was best for her to know."

"That was scary."

"Yes it was, but she needed to know the truth. I was already five and a half months pregnant. That was the scariest moment of my life."

"Mama?"

"Yes, Melissa."

"How did Daddy take it?"

"He took it a little hard, but at the same time, so did his family, but there was no way that we were going to do anything wrong."

"What do you mean?"

"Like having an abortion or giving our baby up for adoption. So we all had to learn how to deal with the situation."

"Wow. Well, Mama, at least you were blessed to know that you had good support."

"Yes, baby, I was. I can't complain at all. That's why I want you to always come to me if you ever have a question. I just don't want you to feel that you are too scared to talk to me. Do you understand, Melissa?"

"Yes, ma'am, I understand." The more my mother talked about her situation, the worse I felt because her situation sounded exactly like mine. I just hoped that I was not pregnant because I could barely take care of myself. The last thing I wanted to do was take care of a baby. I refused to sit here and stress over my situation.

I was really happy when I arrived home. I told my mom that I was tired and I needed to go to my room and take a nap. I just wanted to get away from my mom. I thought she knew more than she was saying, but in the back of my mind, I had some satisfaction because I knew that in less than a week, my period would be on. I would just have to think positive thoughts until then.

I was always told that if a guy wears protection, then there is no way that a female can become pregnant. Especially if the woman's cycle is about to come on. I thought I was in the clear. My friends always used to say that if a woman's period is about to come on, then there is no way that a baby can be conceived. I was going to believe that, no matter how crazy it sounds.

I really hoped that the decision that I made to have sex would not destroy my life. I needed to talk to the Lord one more time:

"Dear Lord, this is Melissa. I need you now more than ever. I just got done having a long talk with my mother. I do not know what she knows about my situation, but what I do know is that I have been praying to you ever since it happened. I need your help to have a clear understanding of what's going on in my life. I am too young to have a child, and I am not ready for one. I feel as if I am a child myself. Deon is trying to go to college so he can have a football career. I just don't want to mess that up for him. He has a scholarship to go to The North Carolina Institute of Athletics, which is one of the best colleges in the city of Raleigh, North Carolina. I am thanking you in advance for your favor on my life, Lord. Amen."

Last night when I was in bed, all I did was talk to the Lord. I asked Him to forgive me, not only for having sex outside of marriage, but for dishonoring my mother's wishes. I know I have a forgiving God. I believe if you ask anything in His name, then you will receive.

As more days went by, the worse I began to feel. I couldn't keep any food down, my face was constantly sweating, and I was getting sick every morning. I had never felt like this before.

One week passed in slow motion as I anticipated my period. Surely, God heard my prayers; His mercy was all I could hope for. I woke up early and quickly went into my bathroom with my pads. I left disappointed because my period was not on.

I went into my room to try to find a calendar to help me remember when my last cycle happened. I was hoping that it would come on. My usual symptoms were not happening, for some reason.

I tried to figure out if March had more days than April; if that is the case, my cycle should come on a day or two later. My nerves were in a wreck.

With this being my last year in high school, I tried to plan out my life, and having a baby was definitely not a part of that plan. I should have thought about that before I had sex.

A week later, I began to see signs that my period was coming on because I was spotting. Now I knew, in a day or two, it will be on full force. "Thank you, God!" I ran quickly into the bathroom and put on a pad. I had never been so happy to put on a pad. Any other time, I hated them. I was so happy to have my period; heck, the people who made the pads should let me be their spokesperson. I would even put my face on the front of the package.

As I was leaving the bathroom, my mother was calling me. She wanted to know where I was.

"I am in the bathroom, putting on my pad."

"Okay."

I guess she wanted to know why in the world I was telling her that; if only she knew. Deep in my heart, I felt she would never know.

The next morning when I went to use the bathroom, I had to do a double take because my period was not on. The pad that I had used was clean. I wiped myself over and over again just to make sure that it was not stuck inside. I was so confused. I just sat there for a while, hoping that the blood forgot to come out, but still nothing happened. Now I was beginning to get nervous all over again.

I thought I might have needed to tell my mother that my period was acting very weird. Maybe I should just wait for at least two more weeks, because there was a chance that my period could have lost track of the time. I never had these problems before. Gosh, but when I had sex with Deon, he did wear a condom, but then again, it was old as heck. I refused to deal with this problem all by myself, so I called Deon. As I dialed his number, I was rehearsing my words. I didn't know what or how to tell him, but he needed to know.

As Deon answered the phone, I paused for a minute. He called my name twice before I said a word.

"Melissa! Melissa! Girl, I hope you are calling me with good news."

"Hi Deon, I don't know how to say this, but yesterday, I had signs of my period coming on. It stayed on for a while, but I don't think that it was my period."

"What do you mean, you don't think it was your period?"

"I was spotting."

"Spotting?" Deon asked.

"Yes, but this morning nothing was there."

"So what are you going to do about it now?"

"I am going to hold off for a couple of weeks and pray that it comes on in the meantime, because I don't know what else to do."

"Melissa, how about I just go to the store and buy you a pregnancy test?"

"Deon, did you just say a pregnancy test! You know I am not ready for all that. I am so afraid to find out if I am really pregnant. It even keeps me up at night to the point where I am constantly tossing and turning. It even affects how I eat because I can barely keep my food down."

"Melissa, I'm sorry."

"Don't be sorry, just continue to pray! That's all I know to do."

"I just want you to realize that we will get through this. I guess I will wait another day or two and then go to the store and get the pregnancy test."

"Okay Deon, whatever you want to do."

After the second day passed, Deon decided to come over to my house. In his hand was a brown paper bag with my pregnancy test. I told him that I really didn't want to know but I knew what was best for me. I was so glad that my mom had left to go and visit her friend. This gave me plenty of time to take the test.

As Deon and I were in the bathroom waiting on the results, I asked him, "What if I am pregnant?"

"Melissa, if you are pregnant, then we only have one option, and that is to do our best to take care of it."

"But Deon, I don't know if that will be the best thing for us. You have to think; you have a college scholarship, and I don't want you to mess up your life."

"I know, but my life will not be messed up as long as I spend it with you."

"Wow Deon, you are so sweet and special."

"Thank you, but I do have a confession to make."

"What is it, Deon?"

"I told my mother that we had sex."

"You did what?"

"Yes, I did. I told her a week after prom because I had a dream that you were pregnant, and I just couldn't keep something like that from my mother."

"Okay, so now you tell me! And I didn't tell my mother yet. I can't believe you. You could have at least told me that you discussed this with your mother. I am outraged! Now I'm the only one who's keeping a secret."

"I know, baby, but I just didn't think that was the appropriate time to tell you. That is why I am telling you now."

"So what did she say?"

"Well, at first she was upset. But she did say that she will be there for us if you're pregnant. I told her that we weren't sure yet, but I was going to the store to get a pregnancy test, and as soon as I found out, I would let her know."

"Now your mother probably thinks differently of me. Thanks a lot!"

As we were finishing talking, we both looked at the test at the same time. I had to take a double look.

Deon nudged me. "Melissa, are you okay?"

"Deon, does that test have two lines? Am I seeing right?"

"Yes, Melissa, it does have two lines."

"Do me a favor and read the directions again. Please make sure two lines mean that I am not pregnant."

"Well, Melissa, I don't have to read the box because I have already read it in the store, and two lines means that you are pregnant!"

"Oh my gosh, Deon! I don't know what I am going to do. How am I going to tell my mother this? I know she will be very disappointed in me. I don't know what to do! I just don't know. At least your mother knows. Please, God, help me with this situation. I need you to speak for me and through me. My mother has been too good to me, and now, I'm going to disappoint her with a baby. I just can't do it. Lord, please protect me."

While I was talking to God, tears were just flowing from my eyes.

"Everything is going to be alright, Melissa," said Deon.

"No, it's not; you don't know my mother like I do."

"That may be true, but I know her well enough."

"Whatever, Deon!"

He held me in his arms and told me that he loved me; he promised me over and over again that everything was going to be okay. I wanted so badly to believe him but I just couldn't. While Deon and I were in the bathroom, I heard the front door open. I knew it was nobody but my mom. I didn't have any other choice but to tell her.

As we walked out of the bathroom, I was holding the test in my hand. I was stunned to see my mother and Deon's mother standing in the hallway together. I almost fainted, because not only did I have to tell my mother, but I also had to tell Deon's mother.

As I glanced at my mother, she had a very disturbing look on her face. She reached down and took the pregnancy test out of my hands. I wanted so badly to run and never look back. But that wouldn't solve anything. She gave me a hug and told me that she loved me, and we would all work this out. I told her that I was so sorry.

My mother said that everything was going to be okay. She had already known that I had sex because Deon's mother told her that there was a possibility that I could be pregnant.

It all became clear to me, at that moment, why my mother was asking me all of those questions. I had no idea that she knew, but I was so relieved that it was finally all out in the open. Thank you God!

My best friend Jessica

After it was all said and done, I was happy that I found out when I did because I was still able to fit into my graduation gown. The best part was that no one could tell that I was pregnant. I just didn't want anyone to talk negatively about Deon and me.

About a month after graduation, Deon decided to go to a college that was closer to home.

He told me that he just couldn't leave me alone while being pregnant. He felt that he would be less of a man to have the woman he loved taking care of his child by herself. I always told him that I was going to be okay because he was only going to be two hours away. He didn't want to hear that. Deon didn't want me raising his child all alone, because he saw how his mother had to struggle to raise him by herself. He said that he refused to have that type of upbringing for his child. I saw that I couldn't win this argument. I was just happy that God gave me a good man.

Four months passed; I was now six months pregnant. I was starting to show a little bit. I knew that I couldn't keep it a secret any longer. But before I let anyone else know, I had to tell my best friend, Jessica. I probably should have told her earlier, because she was my best friend. Being pregnant was not something I was going to broadcast. I just hoped that she would not be mad at me for long, if she got mad at all, but I was sure that she would understand.

Later that day, Jessica came over to my house.

"Hey Jessica."

"Hey, what's up, Melissa?"

"Nothing much, I have something very important to tell you, but I don't know how."

"Just say it, Melissa."

"Okay, I am pregnant."

"Say what? Did you just say that you were pregnant?"

"Yes, that's what I said. I am pregnant."

"But how can that be the case when you are a virgin? We both made a vow to each other that we would not have sex until we were married."

"You're right, Jessica. I realize that I made a mistake. But I only did it one time."

"One time, Melissa? It takes more than just one time to get pregnant, doesn't it?"

"No, Jessica, that's what I thought too, but we were both wrong. The only time I had sex was the night of prom."

"Wait a minute. I thought you were at prom the entire time."

"No, I was not there the entire time. Deon and I left early because he had gotten bored, so we went to go for a walk on the beach, and that is when it happened."

"It, Melissa?"

"Yes, it, Jessica."

"So you two had sex on the beach?"

"No, not on the beach, but in his car."

"You are nasty for that, Melissa."

"Hold on, my intentions were not to have sex with him. It was something that just happened."

"So why did you do it if you were not trying to have sex?"

"I don't know, Jessica. I just got caught up in the moment."

"Yeah, I guess so."

"Look Jessica, I am only here to apologize for not keeping my word. The deed is done; it cannot be erased."

"I understand, Melissa. I am not here to judge you or make you feel bad about your decision."

"I appreciate that, Jessica. I have already asked God and my mother for forgiveness, so I am at peace with it."

"Well, Melissa, it must be in God's will for you to be pregnant. I am a little upset, but that won't last long."

"Yeah, you're right, but if you don't want to continue to be my friend, then I understand."

"I'm not going to be upset forever, Melissa; you can always count on me being your friend because I have been your friend since we were in elementary school. Your mom is basically like a mother to me, and that is something that I will never give up."

"You are most definitely right, Jessica. We have been there for each other for the longest."

"Yes, I was there when your father died. That was a difficult time in your life and I will not stop being your friend just because you are pregnant."

"You don't realize how badly I needed to hear that, Jessica. That means a lot to me. I miss my dad so much."

"I know you do, Melissa."

"Throughout the years, I've been trying to stay strong, but there is not a day that goes by when I don't think about him. I know he is here at all times because I still smell the scent of his cologne, and whenever Deon and I kiss, he knows that he can't kiss me on my right cheek because that was my father's favorite cheek to kiss."

"I love you so much, Melissa."

"That means a lot to me. I love you too and I know that with God's help, we will get through this together."

"Amen," replied Jessica.

Catherine

It's January 11th. The time had finally come for me to give birth, and I didn't realize how excited I was until that moment. My mom and Deon's mom were taking pictures while Deon was holding my hand. He was trying his best to coach me. I was in labor for five hours and it seemed as if I would never have the baby.

About 30 minutes later, I heard a knock on the door. It was my brother Robert Jr. and my best friend Jessica. I was so happy to see them. They both gave me a hug and told me that they loved me.

The time was finally here; my water broke! The pain was so unbearable. I repeatedly asked the nurse for pain pills, but nothing seemed to work. I was yelling at anyone who said a word to me. My mom started rubbing my feet and told me that everything was going to be okay, while Deon had a wet cloth rubbing my face. He was telling me how much he loved me. I knew he loved me, but that was the furthest thing from my mind. All I wanted was to have my baby.

Thirty minutes later, I realized that the baby was finally coming!

"Mama, get the doctor!"

Deon was telling me to calm down.

"You calm down! How can you tell me to calm down? I am the one having the baby, not you!"

"I didn't mean it like that, Melissa."

"Okay, then how did you mean it, Deon?"

"Never mind, baby."

Deon's mother told him to move and give me some space because she sensed that I was getting angry.

As the doctor came into the room, I was already pushing. I couldn't wait any longer. He quickly put on his gloves and told me to take my time and push. "I know he didn't just tell me to take my time," I thought. He is about to hear something that might not be so polite.

Jessica held my hand and told me to push. I told her, "I am pushing." I just didn't know where all these people were coming from, trying to tell me how to have my baby. I thought my mom saw the frustration on my face and told everyone but Deon's mom to sit down. They both stood by my side and coached me along the way. Deon just stood by the side, watching as the baby was coming out.

I saw Deon's eyes grow huge, and I really didn't know what his problem was. Then I heard him say, "What in the world!"

That's when Robert Jr. stood up and said, "Oh my goodness! Do you see that?"

I guess seeing a baby come out really brings out a different side in people. Jessica told both of them to sit down and stop acting like a bunch of children.

After what seemed like forever, I could finally feel the baby coming out. My mother was yelling, "It's a boy! It's a boy, Melissa. We have us a baby boy." I had a huge smile on my face because I was so happy. The more I pushed, the more I felt the head, then his shoulders.

I was wondering how my mother knew the sex of the baby so soon. She began to pause for a second, and then she walked to take a closer look at the baby. She had this puzzled look on her face, and that's when I knew there was a problem. I was hoping my son had all of his fingers and toes. My mother looked at me and said, "Melissa, I am very sorry, but it's not a boy."

"What? So that means it's a girl, but Mother, you just said that I was having a boy."

"I know, I thought it was a boy because your baby doesn't have any hair."

"Are you sure it is a girl?"

"Yes, we are pretty sure," said Deon's mother.

"Sorry for the mistake, Melissa."

"Oh, that is no problem, Mother. This is the happiest time of my life."

I smiled at my mother and that was the moment when she started to cry.

"I love you, Mother."

"I love you too, Melissa."

"But Mother, can you do me a favor?"

"Yes, Melissa?"

"Next time, please let the doctor tell me the sex of my baby," I said with a smile.

"I sure will, baby." Everyone in the room started laughing, even the doctor.

Deon was so excited because he was able to cut the umbilical cord. He was also nervous at the same time because he was shaking. His mom was kissing the baby and said that she was so beautiful. There was not a dry eye in the room; this day was truly a blessing. We decided to name her Catherine, after my dad's mother. She weighed 7 pounds and 9 ounces, and was a big bundle of joy! I could do nothing but thank the Lord for this blessing.

Six months later, Catherine weighed 23 lbs. Her doctor told me to be careful because she was a little overweight for her age. I guess feeding Catherine baby food and oatmeal made her gain a lot of weight. I knew it was probably too early for her to eat cereal, but she was always hungry. Every time she cried, my mother would always tell me to feed her. I trusted my mama's wisdom, so I blamed her for Catherine's baby fat!

Soon afterwards, Catherine started crawling. I was very happy because I could see her growing and learning to do different things. Every time she would do something different, I would write it down in her baby book.

I was so glad whenever Deon would come over to the house, because Catherine would smile and jump for him. That let me know that she loved her dad. He would give her more attention than he would give me, but I didn't mind, because he loved his baby girl. Sometimes, his mother would come and keep her for the weekend. I didn't have to worry about anything, because I had the support of my mother, Deon's mother, and Jessica. I was even able to take correspondence college courses. I had not gotten to the point where I could be away from the baby for more than a few hours. I was so happy for Deon because he already had a year and a half of college out of the way. Like I always said, "God is good!"

Christmas

A year later, Deon and I had a bond that was stronger than ever. Catherine had been walking and talking for the past six months, and she was getting into everything in sight. My baby was a busy body.

I was excited because it was around Christmas time, and that meant Deon would be coming home from school for about a month for the holiday break. Deon and his mother wanted to keep Catherine for about a week or so. At first, I didn't want her to leave me for that long, but at the same time, I needed a break.

It was hard the first night that Catherine was gone. I couldn't sleep because I thought I kept hearing her crying. But the second and third night, I got used to it and I didn't have a problem at all. I knew that she was in good hands, and I could use the extra sleep.

The next day was Christmas Eve. Deon and I had to do a little last-minute shopping for ourselves and Catherine. Our baby had so much stuff that it felt like we were buying for three children, but you only live once.

After we were finished shopping for Catherine, Deon decided he wanted to get his mother a gift. He decided that he wanted to buy her a ring, so we went into the jewelry store to see what we could find. There was only one problem; we didn't know her ring size. He asked me to try on a ring because my hand was about the same size as his mother's. He picked out a gold ring and with three diamonds in the middle.

"Wow Deon, this is a very pretty ring."
"Do you think my mom will like it?"
"I know she will like it because we both have similar taste."
"That's good. I think this is the one then!"

After we were done shopping, we decided to get something to eat. While we were waiting on our food, Deon seemed to be acting a little strange. He began to stare at me.

"Deon, are you okay?"

"Oh, sorry, yeah I'm fine."

"Well, I hope so because you are not acting like yourself."

"Yeah, I'm good, baby. I love you."

"I love you too, Deon."

"Melissa, I want you to know that no one will ever take your place in my heart because you are very special to me."

"Wait a minute, Deon. Where are you getting all of this from? Is something wrong?"

"I just don't want to do anything that would cause you to leave me."

"Leave you? Look, Deon, I will not leave you. I love you so much and you are a great father to our child, plus you are a wonderful man to me. I would be less than a woman to leave a good man like you. Baby, it is not easy to find a man who will love a child and its mother. It is sad to say, but a lot of men will get a woman pregnant, and then they will leave her."

"You are right, baby. Thanks for those words because they really mean a lot to me."

"No problem, baby. I believe it comes from us praying daily and asking God to keep our relationship strong, and plus, we have not had sex since the first time. So far, we have made sure that we will hold off on sex until we get married."

"You are right, Melissa. Sex is not the answer."

"Amen."

It was Christmas Day! My mother, Robert Jr., and I decided to spend Christmas Day with Deon and his mother at their house. My mother stayed up all night cooking dessert while Robert Jr. and I wrapped gifts. It was just like old times. Robert Jr. and I reminisced about our mother and father. Christmas was one of the hardest times for the both of us because that was when my parents would spend a lot of time in the kitchen together. My mom would do the majority of the cooking while my dad would wrap the gifts. My father always wanted to be the one to make the desserts. My mother would try her best to talk him out of it, because that was her specialty. But my father wouldn't take no for an answer. My brother and I used to laugh at them because this would happen year after year.

    I can remember one time our parents were in the kitchen cooking, and Robert Jr. and I were being nosy, trying to pull the tape off all the gifts. We knew that there was one particular gift we both wanted and we just couldn't wait until dinner was done. So we hurried and looked through all the gifts just to find out if our parents bought my favorite doll or if they brought Robert Jr.'s favorite toy gun. We were both a little disappointed because those special gifts were not under the tree. After we were done eating, Robert Jr. and I decided to go into our rooms and lie down. Our parents asked us why we were leaving because it was time to open the presents. We told them that we just weren't in the mood, and asked if we could wait until later. We remembered our mother and father looking at each other with smiles on their faces, but we had no clue why. They asked us if we were okay. We both replied with "yes" and my brother asked them why they asked. My father told him because he saw us looking through the gifts. Robert Jr. and I couldn't do anything but look at each other with blank expressions because we knew that we were busted! Our father told us to go ahead and take a nap while he played with Robert's gun and my mother played with my favorite doll. We both turned around and quickly gave our parents a big hug. We were so happy and this was the best Christmas we ever had.

    Robert Jr. and I decided to load up the car while my mother finished cooking. I was so excited because this was Catherine's second Christmas, and I felt that she would know a little more about gifts than she had last year.

    As we pulled up at Deon's house, he and his mother came to the door and asked us if we needed any help. Robert Jr. yelled at Deon,

"Yes, come help me unload all these gifts while Mama and Melissa get the food!"

As I walked into the house, I saw my baby playing in her play pen. She was jumping up and down, saying "Mama, Mama." I was so happy to see her. I quickly went into the kitchen to put the food down so I could go and get my baby. I never thought I would have missed her so much.

While our mothers were in the kitchen prepping the food for dinner, Deon and Robert Jr. were getting the gifts organized. That was a tradition that my family would do every year. It made it quicker for us to know how many gifts we would each be getting. Catherine had the majority of the gifts.

After we finished eating our Christmas dinner, it was time to open our gifts. Everyone was so happy and thankful for what they received. It took Catherine at least an hour to open all of her gifts. She was very excited to see all of her presents.

As everyone was finishing unwrapping their gifts, I asked Deon where was the gift that he had gotten for his mother? He looked at me and said, "Oh yeah, I have it right here. I just wanted to make sure everyone was done, so I could present the gift."

Deon made a clean spot in the living room.

"Melissa, come up here with me to present this."

"I don't want to, Deon; this is your special gift for your mother, so I think you should do it by yourself." I looked over at my mother; she had a smile on her face and I said, "Mama, why are you smiling because I don't think it is funny. He wants me to stand with him while he presents his mother with a ring that he bought her. This is not funny, Mama." Despite all that I had just told her, the smile still remained on her face. Deon stood in front of the fireplace with a chair by his side. He asked me to at least sit in the chair. Just to keep the confusion down, I agreed to it.

Deon took the ring out of the bag and got down on one knee. I looked at him, wondering if he was alright. He looked into my eyes, and said, "Melissa, this ring that I bought yesterday was not meant for my mother, but for you."

"For me?" I asked.

"Yes, Melissa, I love you. And I want you to know that I will give you the world if I could. I did a lot of praying on this, and I am convinced that we are made for each other. I want you to know that I cannot live one day without you, so with that being said, Melissa, with the blessing of your mother and your brother Robert Jr., would you be my wife?"

"Oh my goodness, Deon, are you serious? You want me to be your wife. Mama, did you already know about this?"

"Yes, baby," said my mother.

"Robert, I am going to get you for this. You know we tell each other everything," I told my brother with a smile and tears in my eyes.

Deon's mother told me that she would not have it any other way. Catherine was smiling, holding a rose in her hand.

I just couldn't hold it in any longer. I stood up and told Deon, "Yes, I would be honored to be your wife. I love you more than words can explain. You have been a very special person to me from the very first moment I saw you. Deon, I would be very crazy to stand here and tell you no. I have been waiting for this moment to come for a very long time."

Deon grabbed my hand and said, "Melissa, I love you," and then he gave me a big hug.

I held him very tightly and I told him, "I love you too."
Thank you, God, for blessing me with this wonderful man in my life.

The wedding

Six months later, Deon and I were planning our wedding and it was beginning to become very stressful. We both decided not to have a huge wedding, just something short and simple, because all we wanted was to be married. So we agreed to go to the justice of the peace with the support of our mothers, Robert Jr., our baby Catherine, and Jessica. We didn't need anyone else because we felt those were the people who matter the most.

Initially I was nervous about getting married because all I could think about was my mother and my father. I could remember my mother always saying that she wanted to grow old with my father, and maybe there would be a chance of them dying together. That is something that never happened because my dad died much too soon.

Sometimes, I wonder if that will ever happen to Deon and me. I really don't want to lose him, because I love him very much. But with my faith in God and constant prayer, there is a good chance that it will never happen to us. I will love Deon until the day I die. I believe his love for me is equally strong. I want our love to endure.

I could not believe it; it was finally our wedding day. I was very excited because I knew that I was going to be Mrs. Deon Sawyers. I couldn't ask for too much more. I was also relieved because Deon, Catherine and I were going to have the same last name.

As I was walking down the aisle, Robert Jr. was by my side to give me away. I knew that since my father could not be there, he would most definitely want Robert Jr. to be the one to do the honors. As Robert, Jr. took me by the arm to escort me down the aisle, I knew he must have been thinking about our father. Daddy always expected Robert, Jr. to be the man of the house when he was away.

As I looked into my brother's eyes brimming with tears, I thought about how much Robert, Jr. actually looked like our father.

"Melissa, you look beautiful. Daddy would be so proud of you if he were here right now. Deon is a good man who is going to be blessed to have you as his wife."

"Thank you, Robert," I replied.

"Are you ready to do this?" Robert, Jr. asked.

"Let's go!" I replied.

Before we said our vows, Deon had asked if he could read his own vows, because he had taken the time to write them for me. I was surprised because he never told me that he was going to do that, plus I didn't have one for him. After I was finished repeating my vows, Deon prepared to read his.

He grabbed my hand and said, "Melissa, I never thought that I would be so happy at this point in my life, but when I found you, I knew you were the one that I wanted to spend the rest of my life with. I feel like everything we did in the past to get us to this point was for a purpose. I would not trade it for anything in the world. I love you with all my heart, mind, and soul. I always dreamed of having a princess in my life but I never thought that God would have given me a queen. I am so happy to have you in my life. Baby, thanks for everything, and I love you."

After Deon was finished saying his vows, I could not stop crying. I never knew that God would have given me someone as special as Deon, at least not this early in my life. I guess I had to go through the death of my father and he had to go through the abuse with his father, just to know what real love really means.

As soon as we were done, the minister told Deon to 'kiss the bride'. I was so embarrassed because Deon would not stop kissing me. I had to tell him, "Baby, that's enough. Let's save some for later tonight!"

While we were standing outside of the courthouse talking, I looked across the yard. I asked Deon if he knew that strange person who was standing in the distance. He was about two hundred yards away, but he was watching every move we made. As Deon looked up, he said, "Oh my goodness, Melissa, he looks like my father."

"Your father, Deon? Are you sure?"

"I'm not completely sure, but hold on and let me ask my mother."

"Hey Mom, can you please come over here for a minute?"

"Yes, Deon?"

"Do you see that person standing over to the left of us?"

"Yes, Deon, I do."

"Is that my father?"

"Yes, it is."

"Mother, are you going to be okay?"

"Oh yes, Deon, baby I am just fine. I just talked to your father briefly about a month ago. He came by the house after he had gotten out of jail."

"Really, Mom?"

"Yes, Deon, at first I was nervous, but there was a police officer with him, so I was okay. All he wanted to do was check on us and make sure that we were alright."

"Was that all, Mama?"

"Yes, baby, that is it. I will always have feelings for your father, but getting back with him is definitely out of the question. I love the way my life is going right now, and I don't want to go through that abuse and pain ever again."

"I understand, but I don't want either of us to have to hurt like that again."

"He just wanted to come by to apologize to the both of us for what he had done in the past."

"Oh really, well what did you tell him?"

"I told him that we both accepted his apology, because if we didn't, then God would not forgive us."

"Okay, so how did he know about my wedding?"

"I thought that you would never ask. We had a conversation about two weeks ago and he told me that he really wanted to see you and his new daughter-in-law. I told him that might not be a good idea because I know how you feel towards him. So I suggested for him to come but stand far away. Really, I wanted you to make your own decision about seeing him."

"Mama, I understand. I feel that you weren't trying to hurt me. You were only trying to help and I love you for that."

"I love you too, Deon. Now come here and give your Mama a hug."

I told Deon that was very sweet how he and his mother showed each other love. He told me that he loves his mother with all of his heart.

After about ten minutes, Deon asked me if I was ready to meet his father. The moment that I had been waiting for was finally here. I told Deon that I was more than ready to meet his father.

As Deon and I approached his father, he grabbed Deon immediately and gave him a hug and said, "Son, I am so sorry for the mistakes that I have made in the past. I didn't think about anyone but myself at the time. I just want to know if you could find it in your heart to forgive me because I have already asked your mother for forgiveness and now I need your forgiveness, son."

Deon looked at his father with tears rolling down his face and said, "Yes, I do forgive you, Dad. I am so happy to see that you have allowed God to change your life. I would be dead wrong if I don't forgive you. The situation that I went through not only made me stronger, but it made me a better man."

"Thank you, son, those are the words I have been waiting to hear for quite a while."

"Now, Dad, I would like for you to meet my new wife, Melissa, and our daughter, Catherine."

"It is a pleasure to meet you. Is it okay if I call you Daddy Clifford?"

"I would not have it any other way, Melissa."

"Thank you, and please meet your granddaughter, Catherine."

"Wow, Deon," said Daddy Clifford, "I never thought a girl would look so much like her father. This baby looks exactly like you, and

Melissa, she has your skin tone. Son, she is beautiful. Thank you, Melissa and Deon, for blessing me with a beautiful grand-daughter, and I promise that I will be there for her."

"Well, Daddy Clifford, just remember that God works in mysterious ways."

"Oh, Melissa, yes He does!"

While talking to Deon's father, I had so many tears flowing down my face to the point where my makeup was messed up. It didn't matter because I felt that Daddy Clifford really meant everything that he had just said. With me knowing what Daddy Clifford did to Deon and his mother in the past, I could tell that he was not that same person. I guess going to jail wasn't so bad after all. While he was in jail, Daddy Clifford became humbled. He was led to Jesus through a prison ministry. They encouraged him to read his Bible daily so he would grow in Christ, and he stood there that day a changed and humbled man. Only the power of Jesus can soften a person's hardened heart.

Twins

A year later, Deon and I were in our last year of college, and anticipating our future together and our growing family. A lot had happened since our marriage. I was eight-and-a-half months pregnant with twins. This time around, when I found out that I was pregnant, I knew that I had to find out the exact sex of the baby from the doctor, because the first time, my mother got the sex of the baby wrong. After talking to the doctor, I learned that I was having twin boys. Everyone was excited about the birth of the twins.

Trying to put the nursery together kept me occupied, not to mention Catherine and I had been decorating her baby brothers' room all day long. I was very happy because both of our mothers were so excited about the birth of their grandsons. I was extremely happy because Deon and his mother had developed a healthy relationship with Daddy Clifford. I didn't think anyone could be friends after being abused by someone, but with the help of God, anything is possible.

As Catherine and I were finishing the final touches to the boys' room, I began to experience a very tight feeling around my waist. It felt as if there was a belt that was wrapped very tightly around my waist, so I decided to sit down. I quickly grabbed a chair, hoping that the pain would gradually go away. But it never did, and it only became worse. I asked Catherine to hurry and get me the telephone so I could call my mother and tell her what was going on. I knew that I wouldn't be able to get in touch with Deon because he was at work and he was thirty minutes away, plus my mother could be here in about fifteen minutes. I told my mother that the pain was unbearable and she knew instantly that I was going into labor. My mother told me to hold on so she could call Deon, and ten minutes later, she pulled into my driveway. I was surprised because it usually takes longer than that to get here, and the next thing I knew, Deon came rushing into the house from work with his mother running behind him. He grabbed me and put me into the car and rushed me to the hospital.

As we pulled up, Jessica and Daddy Clifford were standing there waiting for us. I was saying to myself, "Where in the world are these people coming from so fast?" I just didn't understand, but I was so glad to see them. As I was lying in the hospital bed, the doctor came in and he asked me if I was ready to have the babies. I told him, "Yes sir, I am." He decided to check and see how many centimeters I had dilated. He was very surprised because I was already eight centimeters. He told me that I was going to have my babies sooner than I thought, because when he checked me, he felt a baby's head.

My doctor quickly called the nurse and told her to prep me for the birth of my babies. Deon looked at me and wanted to know if it was alright with me if he stood by my side. I told him, "Sure, but make sure you don't get on my nerves this time." Both of our mothers were in the room and I also wanted to have Deon's father in there. Daddy Clifford was ecstatic about being able to see the birth of his grandsons. Jessica decided to stay in the lobby with Catherine.

After the nurse was finished prepping me for birth, not even five minutes had passed before my water broke. That's when I knew, without a doubt, that it was time for me to have my boys. I started screaming and yelling. "Lord, help me get through this process. Father, please give me the strength to make it through this." Deon was great and very supportive. But his dad, on the other hand, was there telling me to try and stay calm because everything was going to be okay.

I looked at Daddy Clifford and asked him, "Did you just say 'stay calm'?"

"Yes, Melissa, if you don't mind, everything will be okay."

"Well, Daddy Clifford, if you don't mind, I would love for you to take a seat across the room, because I don't want to hear your voice right now."

I think being pregnant made me an instant witch, especially at the time of labor. But I was glad to have Deon's mother in my room because she explained to Daddy Clifford that it was best for him not to say a word to me. She also wanted him to know that I didn't mean anything by what I had just said, but she wanted him to be on the safe side and just sit down. Daddy Clifford told her that he understood. He wanted me to know that he really owed me an apology. I told him that it was not a problem and that I had no hard feelings.

After all the screaming, pushing, and pain, it was finally over. I was so proud to be the mother of those two healthy baby boys. My mom was in the room praising God; she kept thanking Him for all His many blessings that He had stored upon us.

It seemed as if my mother had her own church service going on. The only thing that was left was that she needed to take up the money for the collection.

After discussing the names for our babies, we came up with the names, Ernest and Leon. We got the name Ernest from my father's middle name and the name Leon from Deon's grandfather's name on his mother's side. I was so thankful because I was able to have my baby boys naturally. It was a concern because my doctor told me that it was a possibility that I may need a C-section. But with the help of God, I had them naturally. I was extremely pleased because I did not want cuts on my stomach, and the fact that I had been having nightmares of being cut didn't help any. That was my main concern because I was also told that I could not have more than three children if I had a C-section. When I was younger, I always dreamed of having a huge family.

Trying to make ends meet

A year later, Deon and I decided to move to a smaller town because we now had a larger family and we wanted to move somewhere where the cost of living was lower. We knew that we could have depended on our mothers for the money, but we both felt like that wasn't the right thing to do.

It was really hard for me to make that move, because I was going to miss my mother very much, and my mother and I have never been far apart from each other. I had to explain to my mom that it really wasn't so bad, because we were only one hour away.

Our little girl, Catherine, was now four years old and she was entering pre-k. Our twin boys were now walking, and they were keeping me very busy, but I wouldn't give them up for the world. As I was getting them ready for their afternoon nap, I wanted to make sure the house was clean and dinner was cooked because I knew that Deon would be coming home in about 20 minutes. I felt like I just couldn't let my hardworking husband come home without dinner on the table. Once Deon arrived home, he gave me a hug and a kiss and said, "Melissa, I love you and I miss you."

"I love you too, Deon."

"Melissa, have I ever told you that you are so beautiful?"

"Yes Deon, all the time. So what is it that you have to tell me?"

"Well, you know that I am not making the money that I would like to."

"Okay, and your point is?"

"Melissa, this month is one of the worst months for us."

"And why is that?"

"Well, I had to pay some extra bills last month and my check has been cut due to a change in my job's health insurance policy. I'm going to be behind on the bills only for this month."

"Why in the world are we going to be falling behind? I just don't understand what you are trying to say."

"Melissa, listen, instead of me paying $150 a month for insurance, I will be paying $300 a month. So that is why I was telling you that I will have to skip a month on paying our bills."

"There is no way I will let that happen. I refuse to sit here and listen to this. No way are we going to skip a month on paying our bills. If I must, I will go and get me a job. Deon, I just can't put all of this on you. Baby, don't you know we are a team, and we are going to work together. And I want you to know that I love you too much to let us fail."

"Well, Melissa, I hear everything that you have said, but there is no way that I will let my wife work."

"Did you just say the word 'let'? I hope you are not thinking that I am going to let you treat me like a child."

"No, Melissa, I'm not. I just need for you to stay home with the kids. I always told you it's my job to work."

"And you are doing a great job at that, Deon, but…"

"No buts, Melissa. I don't want to hear any more about it but I do have one more thing to say."

"What is it, Deon?"

"I was offered more hours on my job, but I didn't tell them that I would take it."

"Why didn't you tell them?"

"Well, I wanted to come home and talk to you about it first."

"Well, Deon, if you don't want me to work, then we have to do whatever needs to be done. I just can't see us falling behind on our bills. If it is going to take you having to work a few extra hours, then so be it."

"Are you sure, Melissa?"

"Yes, baby, I am sure but I have one question."

"And what would that be."

"What hours are you working?"

"That is where the problem lies. Now you know I'm working from five in the morning and I get off at five in the afternoon."

"Yes."

"Now my schedule will be from five in the morning until three in the afternoon, and then I will go back at six at night and get off at three in the morning."

"Three in the morning! There is absolutely no way that I would let you stay gone from us that long. Do you know that you will not have time to be a father or a husband? What in the world, Deon. I refuse to let it happen."

"If you think about it, I will only be working this shift for about two weeks, and then I will go back to my regular time."

"I just don't know about that."

"Well, Melissa, you just said to do whatever it takes to get the bills paid, right? So will this be okay with you?"

"Not really, but it seems like I don't have much of a choice."

"At this point, baby, I guess you don't."

"This really hurts me, Deon."

"Why does it hurt you? I told you that it will only be for two weeks."

"I'm upset because you just refuse to let me get a job. I don't even want to talk about it anymore. I guess you're right because it sounds to me like I don't have a choice but to let you do it."

"Thank you so much, baby, and believe me, you will not regret it."

"I hope I don't, and what day are you supposed to start this shift?"

"The boss asked me to start in two days."

"Wow, two days? This is such short notice for me."

"I know, baby, but the offer was just given to me today."

"Do whatever you think is right, Deon. I have enough faith in you to believe that you will make the best decision for our family."

"Thank you, Melissa."

"No problem. Just please make sure it is only for two weeks, which should be just enough time to get our bills on track."

"Yes, Melissa, I will definitely make sure."

I had a soft laugh under my breath, and Deon looked at me and asked, "Is everything okay?"

"Oh yes, everything is just fine. I just had a flashback of my mother and father."

"Okay, so what was it?"

"Well, I could remember my mother had finally gotten tired of staying home, especially when my brother and I had started going to school, so she told my father that she would love to go and find herself a job, just so she could have some extra spending money. But my father refused to hear that."

"So what did your mother do?"

"Well, my mom stayed home and took care of us and the house until my dad came home from work each day."

"That is how marriages are supposed to work, babe."

"I know, Deon, but you know what?"

"What, Melissa?"

"What made this situation so funny is that you sounded exactly like my father."

"That is how it is supposed to be, Melissa."

"Yes, Deon, when I was younger, I could always remember saying that I wanted a marriage just like my parents'."

"Well, Melissa, do you think our marriage is like theirs?"

"I have no response to that comment because I was always told that I need to be careful for what I wish for."

"And what exactly is that supposed to mean?"

"Nothing, Deon, just don't worry about it."

"I will worry about it, Melissa, because you are saying something, and I want to know where you are coming from. Are you happy with me?"

"Yes, I'm more than happy. Please don't take what I said and blow it out of proportion. Deon, I love you, but I would also love to get out of the house and find a job."

"I understand your sense of urgency, Melissa, but I want to be the one to take care of the work and you take care of the house. Plus, I would not want my wife working just any old job."

"Well, to tell you the truth, Deon, any job at this point would do. I never signed up to be a stay-at-home mother when I married you, and you have to realize that times are changing; things are not like they used to be."

"I understand where you are coming from, Melissa, but I just wish we would see eye-to-eye on this."

"Deon, if you think about it, there is no way that we can make it on only one income. My job is to be your help mate, and I would appreciate if you would please allow me to do just that. Please, Deon? I'm begging you."

"Okay, you are right, Melissa. You are so right. Tomorrow we will talk a little more about you working just a part-time job. Maybe just a fifteen-hour week, but nothing more than that. I just don't want my wife to have to go out and work. I just feel that you are better in the house."

"Wait a minute, Deon! Did you say I am better in the house?"

"Melissa, I didn't mean it like that. What I meant was that you are a better cook."

"Never mind all of that, Deon; I am just happy that you came to your senses and you are going to reconsider me getting a job."

"Yes, Melissa, I really don't want you to, but I also want you to be happy."

"Thank you, Deon. I love you so much for that."

"I love you too, Melissa."

I began to pray, "Thank you, God. I am so glad that you have answered my prayers and that you gave Deon a change of heart!"

Not two weeks, but two months later, Deon was still working all of those hours that he promised would only last two weeks. At that point in time, I was extremely upset because he had lied to me! I had never been this angry with my husband. I just could not understand his purpose, because all of our bills were paid and we had some extra money to fall back on. I made up my mind that I had enough, and that I was going to let Deon know how I felt when he came home. The clock read 2:30. That meant that I had an hour to get my thoughts together and try to calm down a little bit before I talked to him, but he really owed me an explanation.

I was pacing back and forth around the house, biting my fingernails, getting my thoughts together for what I wanted him to know. I was going to let him know how dissatisfied I was and that I would not take this anymore.

I began to ask the Lord to please help me because I was thinking too hard about what to say to him. Deon made me so angry. Whenever I would bring up the question about me working, he would always jump to another subject. And every time Deon left for work, Ernest and Leon would cry for hours at a time. I just couldn't take this anymore. This has really become a stressful time for me.

An hour later, Deon pulled up into the driveway. I had to make sure I had the right thing to say, because I knew if I didn't ask God to help me, I would have been saying some ungodly words. As Deon opened the door, I greeted him with a smile saying, "Hi sweetie, how has your day been so far?"

"I am very tired, Melissa."

"I understand that, but do you have a few minutes for us to talk, because I have a lot on my chest and I really need to get it off."

"Sure, Melissa, but can you give me a couple of hours because I need to get washed up and take a nap."

"A nap," I replied. "I understand taking a bath, but how can you take a nap when you have been away from us all day? Deon, do you realize that we really don't get to spend much time together anymore? I really miss my husband, and our kids miss their father. I never thought for a moment that this was going to happen. I am really missing you, Deon. I don't know if you can understand that."

"I know you do, Melissa. And I miss my wife also. But I just need to get myself on track."

"On track? Deon, we have been on track for the last month. How much more track do you need to get yourself on? Is there something that you are not telling me?"

"Oh, Melissa, it's nothing."

"Okay, Deon, I really hope it's not."

"You know what?"

"What, Deon?"

"Just give me a little time and things will be back to the way they used to be."

"You know what, since you are my husband, I am going to believe you."

"Thank you, Melissa, that's all I'm asking from you. Now give me a kiss. I love you, baby."

"Go ahead and take your bath because the water is getting cold."

"Thank you for running my bath water for me, baby."

"No problem. Anything for you."

Seeking my mother's advice

As Deon went to take his bath, I decided to give my mother a call. I just wanted to check on her and see how she was doing. When she answered the phone, I knew that she could tell in my voice that something was wrong. The very first thing she asked me was if everything was alright.

I replied, "Yes, and why do you ask?"

"Because I know you better than you think I do."

"Okay, you got me. It has been about two months that Deon has been working long hours, and I just don't know how much more I can take."

"Melissa, when you say long hours, what exactly do you mean?"

"Well, he would go to work at five-thirty in the morning and then he would get off around three-thirty in the afternoon."

"That's not so bad, Melissa."

"No, Mama, that's not it."

"Okay, what else is it, Melissa?"

"Well, then he would go back at six thirty in the evening and he would get off around three o' clock in the morning."

"Wow, Melissa, I could understand why you would be upset."

"I know, and I really didn't want to call you about our issues, but I really needed someone to talk to."

"Let me tell you something, you know I'm always going to be your mother and you can always call me whenever you need anything. You do know that, right?"

"Yes I do. Mama?"

"Yes, Melissa?"

"Nothing, never mind."

"No tell me."

"He feels like we are falling behind on our bills and that's why he is working like he is. I told him that I could at least go and get a part-time job. At first, he didn't want to hear that, but he told me that we would talk about it the next day."

"So did you two talk?"

"No, we didn't because that was over two months ago, and every time I would bring it up to him, he would jump to another subject. I'm getting frustrated. Mama, you know I never grew up without my father being home at night, and I refuse to let our children grow up without their father being here at night. There is no telling what can happen late at night with no man home, Mama. Someone could try to break into our home or something like that."

"Well, you are right, Melissa. I could understand why you feel that way. I was so thankful to have a man like your father."

"Me too, Mama."

"Melissa, I want to get a little personal with you, if you don't mind."

"Yes, ma'am."

"When was the last time you and Deon had sex?"

"Mama!"

"What, Melissa, you said I could get personal with you. Now answer the question!"

"To be honest, it was one day last week. Deon had an off day and we finally had family time together, and later that night was our time. And Mama, let me tell you, we had a really good time. That was what I really missed. I really missed spending quality time with my husband."

"I know you do, baby. I know you do. Well, you know that you have your money in the account from the settlement."

"Yes, ma'am, I know."

"Have you told Deon about that?"

"No, ma'am, I didn't."

"Why not, Melissa?"

"Because I don't think he would want to touch something that was given to me."

"I don't know about that, Melissa."

"Until God instructs me to tell him, that's when he will know. Mama, I think right now is not the time."

"Wow, Melissa, are you okay, because that sounds kind of selfish?"

"Yes, I am. I don't think he would want any of the money."

"Why do you say that?"

"Because I think he really enjoys working."

"Baby, I think the best thing for you to do is keep your money for emergency purposes only."

"Yes ma'am, thank you so much for the advice, Mama. I really am beginning to feel a lot better now."

"That's good to know. Now, how are my grand-babies doing?"

"Oh, they are just fine."

"I really do miss them."

"Mama, they miss you also."

"I was thinking about coming down one day next week to visit my babies."

"Do you know which day?"

"No, I haven't decided just yet."

"Well, just let me know because I have a doctor's appointment at two o'clock on Wednesday. And I would like to know if it would be possible for you to watch the boys then."

"That is no problem, Melissa. I am more than happy to watch my grand-babies!"

"Thanks, Mama."

"Well, Wednesday it is."

"Okay, I will see you then."

"Don't forget to give my grand-babies a hug and a kiss for me."

"I sure will. See you later."

As soon as I got off the phone, I began to thank God for blessing me with a great mother.

My yearly doctor's examination

A week later, I was cleaning the house because I knew that my mother was on her way over. Plus, I was also getting ready for my doctor's appointment. Hopefully, she would be here shortly. As I was in my room getting dressed, I heard the doorbell ring. I rushed to the door to see who it was. I was so happy because it was my mother. I was so excited to see her because it had been a while since we last saw each other. I kept hugging and kissing her.

"I'm so glad to see you, Mama!"

"Baby, I am so glad to see you too. Melissa, my baby, I want you to know that I really do miss you!"

"Aw, Mama, I miss you too."

"Do you have everything together for the babies?"

"Yes, ma'am, I do. You don't have to worry about feeding the boys, because they have already eaten their lunch. They should be ready to take their nap."

"Their nap?"

"Yes, ma'am."

"Melissa, do you realize that I just drove about an hour to spend time with my grand-babies? There is no way that they will be here taking their nap. Not under my care."

"Mama, they really need their nap."

"Well, when you get back from your doctor's appointment, then they can take a nap."

"Yes, ma'am."

"Thank you, Melissa. I am so glad that you understand."

"Yes, I do, Mama."

"Okay, now you run ahead and go to your doctor's appointment and the boys and I will be just fine. Wait, Melissa, before you go...

What time does my baby Catherine come home?"

"She will be here in about thirty minutes. The bus will put her out in front of the house."

"Okay great, I'll be looking out for her."

"By the way, Mother, she doesn't know that you are here."

"That is perfect because I want it to be a surprise."

"She will definitely be surprised. Okay, I will see you in a few."

"Hey, Melissa?"

"Yes, Mama?"

"Why are you going to the doctor? Is everything alright?"

"Oh yes, Mama, everything is just fine. I just have to get my yearly exam today."

"Baby, hopefully everything is going to be okay."

"I'm sure I am fine. Love you, Mama."

"I love you too, Melissa."

All I kept saying to myself was, "Lord, I don't know what I will do without my mother."

While I was sitting in the waiting room at the doctor's office, I was trying to decide if I needed to call my mother to check on the boys. I just didn't want her to stress out, because they could really be a handful at times.

After a little more consideration, I decided to follow my heart and use the payphone at the doctor's office to call my mom. As the phone started to ring, my mother answered, "Yes, Melissa, how may I help you?"

"Mama, how did you know that it was me? Are you psychic or something?"

"Melissa, I just knew it was you. Plus, I had a strange feeling you were going to call."

"Mama, you are too funny. Well, Mama, I was calling…"

"No, Melissa, don't tell me!"

"What, Mama?"

"Are you going to tell me that you are calling to check on the boys? Please don't tell me that you are calling me for that."

"Mama, it is not like that."

"Well, Melissa, you tell me what it's like."

As I began to talk, my mother interrupted me, saying, "Never mind, Melissa, please don't tell me. I am just surprised that you are calling me for this."

"Mama, I know how the boys can be. I just didn't want them to stress you out."

"Listen, Melissa, if I was able to put up with you and Robert Jr., I know that I would be able to put up with anybody, especially my own grand-kids."

"Wow, Mama, I didn't think about it like that. You know what, I am very sorry."

As my mother started to giggle, she replied, "I will forgive you this time."

"Thank you, Mama. I've got to run; they are calling my name."

"I love you, Melissa."

"I love you too, Mama. See you in a few."

"Okay."

As Nurse Miwon called my name, I had to go to the restroom to take a urine test. I never could understand why they would make you pee in a cup, when I was only coming for a yearly checkup.

As Doctor Jerome entered my room, he said, "Hi Melissa, how have you been?"

"Hi, Doctor Jerome, I am doing just fine, besides my boys keeping me real busy."

"I bet, Melissa. It is hard enough having one baby, but it is harder trying to raise twins."

"You are right."

"Okay Melissa, I'm going to need you to lie down on your back and put your legs on the leg guards, if you don't mind."

"Yes, sir."

"You might feel a little pressure, so please be careful not to tense up too much."

"Oh, no problem."

"Well, Melissa, is there anything new going on in your life?"

"New? Like what, Doctor Jerome?"

"Well, Melissa, I haven't seen you in a while, so I just want to know what's been going on with you."

"Everything is okay, but it could always be better."

"I could understand that. But what do you mean by better?"

"Well, you know my husband, Deon, right?"

"Yes, I do. As a matter of fact, I have known him for the past five years."

"Yes sir. Well, he has been working a lot of hours and I'm so frustrated with him."

I guess the doctor was so interested in hearing about my life that he forgot that he was dealing with me in a delicate area.

"Ouch, Doc! That hurts."

"I am sorry, Melissa."

"No problem. Well, like I said, it is hard for me to raise my babies when their father is not home much."

"Well, Melissa, you have to think like this, at least you have a man that works. Right?"

"Yes, you are right. But I would also love a man who would give me a little more attention."

"Well, Melissa, all I can do is tell you to pray. God is the only one that can change this situation for you."

"You are definitely right about that."

As the doctor was finishing up the procedure, Nurse Miwon entered the room with a piece of paper, and she handed it to Doctor Jerome. He stood up out of his seat and said, "Interesting!"

With a puzzled look, I sat up and asked, "What is so interesting?" Doctor Jerome and Nurse Miwon looked at each other and began to laugh. I said, "That is enough. Can you all please tell me what is so funny, because maybe I want to laugh too?"

"Well Melissa," said Doctor Jerome, "I don't know if this is going to make you want to laugh but here it goes." It seemed like it took forever for him to say what he had to say but all I heard was, "You are pregnant."

"What did you just say?"

"Look here, these are the results of the pregnancy test you just took when you came in today."

I looked at the paper and saw the proof before my very eyes. However, I still couldn't believe it, so I asked, "I have tested positive on my pregnancy test?"

"Yes."

"But I didn't come here for a pregnancy test!"

The doctor began to explain. "Melissa, whenever you come to get your yearly exam, we automatically test you for that."

"Oh my gosh. Not again!" I said.

"What's wrong? I thought you would be happy."

"I knew I had always wanted more babies but definitely not now."

"Oh well," said Nurse Miwon, "it looks as if you don't have any other choice now."

"I guess you are right. But I don't know if this will change Deon."

"What do you mean change?"

"Never mind."

"Why are you trying to change him?" said Nurse Miwon.

"I just wish that he would decide to stay home with the kids and me."

"Melissa, somebody has to work."

"Yes, you are right, but at least he could work less hours. I don't think I'm asking for too much. All I'm saying is that I just can't raise all of these babies alone."

"Well, I can agree with you on that," said Nurse Miwon.

"Well, thank you very much, at least someone understands."

"Okay now, Melissa," said Doctor Jerome.

"Yes sir?"

"Let's get back to the fact that you are pregnant."

"Okay."

"How do you think your husband is going to feel about this?"

"Well, Doctor Jerome, I can't answer that because he is already working a lot of hours. He is trying very hard to maintain all the bills, so at this point, I really can't answer you. I guess it's because I am trying to absorb all of this."

"What do you mean, Melissa?" said Nurse Miwon.

"Well, I'm surprised that I am pregnant."

"How can you be surprised, Melissa? You know how easy it is for you to get pregnant."

"I know, but Deon and I haven't made love in a while. I know this might not sound right, but we only had sex three times within the last month."

"Melissa, are you listening to yourself talk?"

"Yes, I told you that it might sound crazy."

"You're right because you are talking foolish."

"Nurse Miwon, can you explain why you are saying that?"

"Melissa, you have been coming to us for the past five and a half years."

"Okay and what does that have to do with anything?"

"I can remember when you first came to this office."

"Do you remember that first visit, Melissa?"

"Yes."

"I remember that you were surprised because you were pregnant."

"Yes, ma'am, I really was, and I was very scared when Deon came over with the pregnancy test from the convenience store. I was so surprised about the results because I didn't want to be pregnant."

"I can understand that, especially with you being at a young age."

"Not only that, but I didn't want to disappoint my mother or myself."

"But you are older now, Melissa, and an experienced mother. I don't think your husband will be upset with you or the situation."

"Nurse Miwon, you are right."

"I can remember, back then, you were telling me that you two only had sex one time."

"Yes, it was. I guess I have been under so much stress that I was not thinking, and by me shutting my mouth and listening to you, I realize that I was talking crazy. Everything you said to me is making so much sense. Talking it out has really helped me process all of this.... Thank you."

"I am glad to hear that, Melissa."

"Yes, ma'am, back then I was a virgin. I slipped up one time and that was all it took for me to get pregnant. I have to remember that anything is possible."

"You are right about that!"

"Well, if you don't mind, could you please make me a copy of this paper so I can take it home to Deon?"

"Yes. As a matter of fact, you can take this one."

"Thank you."

"You're welcome and I'm going to give you my personal number so that you can reach me at any time if you need someone to talk to."

"Yes, ma'am, and I appreciate it."

"No problem. I feel like I have a bond with you, and I don't want you to feel like you have to go through this all alone."

"I really appreciate it, but I shouldn't have to go through this alone because I have a great husband who will not let that happen."

"I hope not. But I want you to keep my number just in case."

"Yes, ma'am, I will."

"Okay, Melissa," said Doctor Jerome.

"Yes sir?"

"When you go up to the front counter, I want you to make sure that you make an appointment with me no later than two weeks from today."

"Yes sir, I sure will."

"Okay and I will be praying for you and Deon."

"And I will do the same," said Nurse Miwon.

"I am so thankful for the two of you. I just don't know what I would do without you."

"Well, Melissa, you are very special to the both of us."
"Thank you very much."
"You are quite welcome."
"I will see you in about a week or two."
"Thank you."
"No. Thank you, Melissa. And by the way-"
"Yes?"

"Just remember our God is good. Like in Romans 8:28, which promises that all things work together for the good of those who love God. And who are called according to His purpose. Melissa, I know you love God and you and I both know that you are called according to His purpose. Everything is going to work out for your good."

"Oh yes He is!"

As I was traveling back to my house, I wondered what would be the best way for me to tell Deon. I had been rehearsing for the past thirty minutes, but I just couldn't seem to get it right with all of the stressing and talking to myself. Finally, I had come up with my answer in the back of my mind and it was to just say it. I couldn't argue because it made so much sense and I was going to have to tell him sooner or later. Plus, it is not like Deon is my boyfriend and I am just shacking up with him. He is my husband. It's right in God's eyes, and he should be very happy because I know that I am. I felt that this might make my baby stay home with us, or at least work less hours. All I could do was just hope.

Deon was already home when I got there. "Lord, I hope he is not sleeping." As I walked into the house, my mother and Catherine were playing. They were holding hands and going around in circles. Until Catherine spotted me and began yelling, "Mommy, Mommy, you're home! I miss you so much."

"I miss you too, Catherine."
"Mommy, look who's here. It's Granny."
"Baby, I see."
"Hey, Mother, where are the boys?"

"They were very tired so I decided to put them to sleep. I knew they weren't going to last much longer."

"Oh, okay."

"So how did your doctor's appointment go?"

"It went well."

"Where is Deon?" I asked.

"He's in the bedroom."

"I'm going to talk with him and I will be back in a few."

"No problem, take your time. We will be right here."

"Okay, Mother."

While I was in the bedroom, Deon was in our bathroom taking a shower. Once Deon was done, he walked into the bedroom with only his towel wrapped around him. I had to catch myself, because if I didn't have anything important to tell him, I would jump all over my baby. But first things first.

"Hey, Deon, how was your day?"

"Hey, Melissa, it was fine. You know, I have been doing a lot of thinking lately."

"Oh you have?"

"Yes, Melissa, I have."

"About what?"

"I know I have been neglecting you and the kids for a while now, and I decided that I will cut back on my work hours and stay home more."

"Deon, are you serious?"

"Yes, Melissa, I am. I love you and my kids too much not to be here."

"Deon, I have been waiting for you to say that for the longest. Thank you so much."

"No, Melissa, thank you. Your mother told me that you had a doctor's appointment today."

"Yes, baby, I did. Don't you remember me telling you that?"

"No, I don't."

"I mentioned it to you about a week ago."

"I'm sorry, baby, but I still don't remember."

"You probably were too tired to remember."

"Well, so how did it go?"

"It went fine, I guess."

"What do you mean, you guess?"

"Well, I won't know the results of my entire test for about a week. Doctor Jerome told me that he is going to send them in the mail."

"Is that all, Melissa?"

"No, I got the results of my pregnancy test."

"Pregnancy test?"

"Yes, Deon, I'm pregnant."

"What! How in the world are you pregnant? Hold on, Melissa, have you been cheating on me?"

"Did you really just ask me if I have been cheating on you? How could you let something like that come out of your mouth! I would never do such a thing. That day when we both said 'I do', I meant just what I said. Now you have really pissed me off!"

"I'm sorry, Melissa. It's just that was the last thing that I was expecting to hear."

"So I guess you don't remember having sex with me, do you? It was only three times this month."

"I know, baby. I was just kidding, and I didn't mean it like that."

"Well, there is no other way that you could have meant it, but don't worry about it."

"I'm a little disappointed because our boys are only a little over a year old."

"I know that, Deon."

"They are both still in pampers. Well, it's like this, Melissa."

"I am listening, Deon."

"Okay, for the past few months, I have been working hard just to make sure we stay above water."

"Deon, please don't tell me that you are going to continue working those hours?"

"I can't tell you that I will completely stop, but I will guarantee one thing."

"And what's that?"

"I will not work as much."

"Thank you, Deon. I really needed to hear that."

"And Melissa?"

"Yes?"

"After this baby, that's it. There is no way that we could afford another one. Melissa, don't get me wrong because I love kids, but they are not cheap."

"Okay, Deon, whatever you say, but guess what?"

"What, Melissa?"

"You know what it takes to have them, right?"

"Yes I do. That's why I am telling you that this will be it. And you know what else, Melissa?"

"What, Deon?"

"I am going to make me a doctor's appointment."

"For what, Deon?"

"I am going to get a vasectomy."

"A what?"

"A vasectomy, you never heard of that?"

"I think I have. Is that when a man gets clipped?"

"Well, Melissa, it goes something like that. It's when a man wants to stop making children. It's something like when a woman has a hysterectomy."

"No, Deon, that is not what that is. A hysterectomy is when a woman may have problems with her body. That is not her choice to have one."

"Well, how do you know what that is, Melissa?"

"Because, my mother had to have it done. Now Deon, women who don't want to have any more children may get their tubes tied."

"Okay, Melissa."

"Now back to you thinking about getting yourself a vasectomy. I don't want you to do that."

"Why not, Melissa?"

"Because I feel that as long as God has put us together, then I don't see anything wrong with having babies."

"Melissa, do you hear yourself talking?"

"Yes, Deon, I do. Listen, if it is the Lord's will to have kids, let's be obedient to Him."

"Well, Melissa, I love the Lord and I may not know him as much as you do. But one day, I will. But I do know one thing."

"And what is that, Deon?"

"The Lord has a lot of other people in this world, and believe me, He could use some of them to make these babies. Do you think He only chose us to do that?"

"Well, I am not going to stand here and listen to you, especially when you are talking nonsense."

"Why are you thinking that it is nonsense, Melissa? I am serious."

"Whatever, Deon. When you consider working less hours and start spending more time with your family and in church, then you can understand how to love the Lord."

"Melissa, you know what?"

"What, Deon?"

"You are right."

"You don't have to tell me that because I know I am right."

"And you know what else, Melissa?"

"What, Deon?"

"I love you."

"I love you too, Deon."

As Deon and I finished talking, I decided to tell my mother the good news. She was very excited because having a lot of children was always my mother's dream. She always wanted to have a large family. With the death of my father, it was not possible. So I guess she's now living her dream through me.

"Mama, I love you and I don't know what I would do without you."

"I love you too, Melissa."

"And Mother?"

"Yes, Melissa?"

"I want to thank you so much for being a loving and caring mother. I really don't know what I would do without you."

"Melissa, I also want to thank you."

"Thank me? For what?"

"Because you have always been a respectful daughter to me, especially since you have become an adult."

"Aw, Mama, you didn't have to say all of that."

"No, Melissa, I truly thank you for being a loving and patient daughter."

"No problem. I learned from the best."

"Oh yes, you did," my mother said with a laugh.

As we finished up laughing and talking, I gave my mother a huge hug. It was very hard for me to let her go. I guess that whenever I am around my mother, I just feel a comfort in my spirit. I thank you, God, for blessing me with a special mother!

A visit from an old friend

Nine months later, it was time for me to have my fourth baby. I was very excited because this time Deon and I decided not to know the sex of the baby. We just wanted to be surprised. I was so happy because Deon kept his word and he had slowed down working all of those hours. He only worked his regular morning shift. Thank goodness.

While I was in my room getting my bags prepared to go to the hospital, I heard a knock on the door. As I looked out the window, I couldn't believe who it was. It was my best friend, Jessica. I opened the door and she greeted me with a hug. I told her that I was so glad to see her.

"I'm glad to see you too, Melissa," replied Jessica. "I just decided to stop by and see you while I was in town. So how are you doing?"

"Great, and where in the world have you been? I haven't talked to you in nine months."

"Never mind where I've been, is that a baby in your stomach?"

"Yes, ma'am, it sure is."

"Why didn't you tell me that you were pregnant, Melissa?"

"I don't know, Jessica. I guess I just was not thinking."

"Melissa, why in the world did you never think about telling your best friend that you are pregnant?"

"I'm sorry, Jessica, I just had so much to do around the house, and with the babies. But you know I always think about you."

"I wonder if you really do think about me."

"What is that supposed to mean, Jessica?"

"I am wondering if you really care for me as a friend."

"How dare you say that? You know I do."

"Well, I sure can't tell!"

"Please, Jessica, don't start."

"Don't start what? You know I'm telling the truth."

"You know what, Jessica?"

"What, Melissa?"

"I'm not going to stand here and argue with you. I refuse to. If you can't come to my home and have a better attitude, I feel that it is best for you to leave."

"No, Melissa, I can't leave."

"And why not, Jessica?"

"I love you."

"Well, I can't tell that you love me! If this is what you call love, then I would hate to see how you may treat your enemies."

"Melissa, I am so sorry, because I know I am also at fault. I shouldn't have stood here and blamed it all on you. I could have called you also, but I didn't. You were right, Melissa, so please, will you accept my apology?"

"Yes, I will accept your apology even though I am mad at you, but you know that I can't stay mad at you for too long."

"I love you, Melissa."

"I love you too, Jessica. Now come with me into my room so I can finish packing my clothes for the hospital tomorrow."

"Tomorrow, Melissa?"

"Yes, I am having my baby tomorrow."

"Wow, I knew God sent me over here for some reason."

"Well, at least you already have your answer. So come on and let's go."

"I am right behind you."

While I was getting my clothes packed, I began having sharp pains running down my back. I told Jessica that I needed to sit down for a minute.

"Melissa, are you okay?"

"Girl, yes, I just think I've been doing too much and I need to rest."

"If you just show me what you need, I can finish packing for you."

"No, Jessica, you don't have to do that for me."

"Melissa, you know I will do whatever you need me to do."

"Okay, Jessica."

"Oh yeah, by the way, where is Deon?"

"At my mom's house. He took the kids over there so she could keep them for a week or two."

"I can't believe you let them leave like that."

"Well, Jessica, I can believe it. You just don't know how much a mother needs a break. It doesn't matter if it is only for a day or two. She is keeping them only because she wants me to focus on the birth of my baby."

"I can understand that."

"Well, Jessica, I hope you do, because whenever God blesses you to have children, you will see what I go through. Until then, just be quiet."

"Be quiet."

"Yes."

"How rude are you?"

"I'm not being rude; I was just kidding."

"You know how our parents were when we were younger. Don't you remember when our parents needed a break?"

"Girl, yes I do. That's when I would stay over at your house or you would stay at mine. Girl, those were the days. I could never understand why they needed breaks. I always said to myself that they get breaks when we go to school. I felt that was a break enough. But, Jessica, now I understand what they were talking about, especially my mother. She was the one who was always home with Robert Jr. and me."

"Yeah, you are right about that."

"Can you believe Deon has me doing the same thing?"

"What do you mean, Melissa?"

"Girl, he has me staying home with the kids, while he is working."

"Wait a minute, are you telling me that he doesn't want you to get a job at all?"

"No, he doesn't! I have tried for the past year or so and he is still being so stubborn, but I can tell you one thing."

"What's that, Melissa?"

"He doesn't work as much as he used to."

"What do you mean by that?"

"Oh, I must have never told you. Well, I don't like telling my business, but I feel that I can trust you."

"Don't go there, Melissa. You know that you can trust me."

"Well, we were falling behind on our bills, and Deon wanted to work extra hours just to get us back on track. He told me that it would only be for no more than two weeks, but it wasn't."

"How long was it?"

"Jessica, it was for over a year."

"A year?"

"Girl, yes."

"Well, how many hours did he work?"

"He worked about nineteen hours a day."

Jessica could not believe what she had just heard.

"What! Did you say nineteen hours?"

"Yes I did."

"Well, how did you handle that?"

"I didn't, but at the same time, I did, with the help of God. I didn't know if I was coming or going. Whenever Deon would get off his first shift, he would come home and eat, take a bath and then take a nap. There were very little intimate moments for the two of us."

"I bet, so how did this little one come along?"

"Well, whenever he would have a day off and he was not so tired, then it would be time for the kids and then me."

"Well, I can tell you one thing, Melissa; I see that you do love him."

"Oh, Jessica, yes I do. He's my baby. I just wished that he would take more time out for his family. But I can say that he has made a huge change since then."

"Why do you say that?"

"Because he no longer works the second shift and he is home more often. Now that the boys are over two years old, he takes them out a lot more to spend time with them."

"Melissa, what about Catherine?"

"She is doing fine. Can you believe she is now in kindergarten?"

"Are you serious?"

"Yes, I am."

"It is so funny how time flies."

"Yes, it is. I thank God every day."

"You should."

"Well, I need to go to the restroom. I will be right back."

"Okay, I will be right here."

"I hope so, Jessica."

"You are too funny, Melissa."

"Ouch!" I screamed.

"Melissa, what's wrong? Are you okay?"

"Yes, I am still having these sharp pains."

As I was taking short breaths, I went into the restroom so I could throw water on my face. I was feeling a little faint, and I suddenly fell to the ground. Jessica ran into the restroom, only to see me on the floor.

She yelled loudly,

"Melissa, get up! Get up!"

"I can't, Jessica," I replied.

She looked down on the floor and saw that my water had broken.

"Melissa, do you know that you have water on the floor?"

"Yes, I do. Jessica, my water just broke."

"What do you mean, your water just broke?"

"I can't talk too much because I am in so much pain, but I am about to have my baby."

"You what? Oh heck no, you are not! Hold on, let me call someone. I am not going to deliver a baby."

"Jessica, you might have no other choice."

Jessica stood up, yelling, "Lord, I don't know how to deliver a baby! Please, Lord, help me."

While Jessica was yelling, she was busy calling 911. As she was talking to the operator, Deon came home.

"Deon, Deon," Jessica was yelling. Deon rushed into the room.

"Hey, Jessica, what are you doing here?"

"Don't worry about me. Your wife is in the restroom and she is about to have her baby!"

"What!" Deon said emphatically.

"The baby?"

"Yes, Deon, she is in labor."

"Move out of the way, Jessica. I need to go and check on her. Melissa. Melissa, baby, are you okay?"

"No, Deon, I am not okay. I am having this baby with or without you."

"Please, Melissa, don't have it yet. The paramedics are on their way."

"I can't hold on. I am having it right now."

"Oh my gosh, I don't know what to do, Melissa!"

"Deon, just go into the closet and get some towels."

"Some towels?"

"Yes, towels!"

"Then what should I do next?"

"You will put the towels underneath me and prop my legs open."

"Melissa, you know I can't do this. I just can't!"

"And why not, Deon?"

"I can't look down there."

"Down where?"

"You know where, Melissa. Baby, you know that I have problems seeing the baby come out of you."

"Oh my gosh, Deon, you didn't have a problem any other time. Well, if you can't help me, then where is Jessica?"

"She is outside waiting for the ambulance to come."

"Well, I think you need to go outside and let her come in here."

"Okay, I sure will."

I began to ask God, "Lord, what have I gotten myself into?"

As Deon was going to the door, the emergency workers were coming in. He quickly led them into the bathroom, as he stood at the door watching. It was a blessing to have them come when they did, because I was able to make it to the hospital in time to have the baby.

During the time they were prepping me, the baby was on its way out. This was the easiest pregnancy that I ever had. It became easier when I made it to the hospital. We were so blessed to have us a brand new baby girl. We decided to name her Nichole. There was no particular reason for her name; it was just the first name that came to my mind, and Deon agreed with me. I think he was just so exhausted that any name would do.

Our precious gift

I thank the Lord for our beautiful blessing. I was so thankful to have some peace of mind. Deon and I had been working very hard together as a team. In the mornings, he would get the boys dressed and he'd take them to school, and then he would go to work. My job was to take care of Nichole, get Catherine dressed, and take her to the bus stop. I could not have it any better, because her bus stop was directly in front of our house.

Five months ago, Deon and I had a very long talk. He brought up the subject again of getting a vasectomy.

I told Deon that there was no way that I would let him do that.

He replied, "Why not, Melissa? Don't you think we have enough children"?

"Yes, Deon, we may have enough, but I am not going to stop God if He continues to bless us."

Deon was furious. "Melissa, are you crazy?"

"No, Deon, I am not crazy. I have learned to trust and depend on God."

"Well, I was always told, Melissa, that God gives you common sense."

"Well, Deon, I never told you that He didn't. But like I said before, I am not going to sign any papers for you to get that done." I just couldn't believe how Deon was acting.

Deon continued, "Well Melissa, if you are not going to agree with me getting a vasectomy, you could at least get on birth control pills."

"Deon, why should I do that? It's not like birth control pills are one hundred percent."

"I know that, Melissa, but at least it could help in some kind of way. It is better for you to take something rather than nothing."

"Okay, Deon, you are right." Just to stop arguing with him, I made a decision to take birth control pills.

"Finally, Melissa, you agree with something that I suggested."

"What's that supposed to mean?"

"Never mind!"

Six months passed while I was on birth control pills. Deep in my heart, I knew that taking birth control pills on a daily basis would be a hard thing for me to do. The smart thing about forgetting to take my pills was I could always double up the next day. I knew that I was playing a very dangerous game, but I was trying to do my best. I sometimes wondered if I made the right decision of telling Deon that he couldn't get the vasectomy done. Lord, I hope I didn't. In a week, Deon and I would be celebrating our fourth wedding anniversary. He had made reservations for the two of us. We were planning on being gone for a whole week. I was so excited! Deon's father was keeping the boys, and our moms would take turns keeping the girls. I had been so excited, because we had not had a night, better yet a whole week, to ourselves since we had our children.

Anniversary trip

I was so excited when it was my anniversary. While I was home packing my clothes, I wanted to make sure I didn't leave anything out of my suitcase. Deon was smart; he had already had his clothes packed days in advanced. I was happy because he was able to pack all of the kids' clothes. As we were loading up the car, Deon had made sure to remind me to get my birth control pills. I was so glad that he did, because I had almost forgotten about them. I also forgot to get my toothbrush off the bathroom sink. Wow, I was losing it! I don't know what I would do without my Deon. After dropping the kids off, we were on our way to our destination. I had been asking Deon for weeks where would we be going, and he told me that it was a surprise. I said to him, "You know I don't like surprises."

He replied, "Well, have I ever done you wrong?"

"No, you haven't."

"Okay then. Just let me surprise my baby for once. I want you to know that I am so grateful to have you as my wife, and if there is anything I can do to show you that, I will. So please don't mess up my groove."

"Your groove? Deon, you are too funny. I didn't know that you had a groove."

"Well, guess what, Melissa."

"What?"

"Now you do."

"Look at you! What in the world am I going to do with you?"

"Baby, if you don't know, I can show you."

"That's my man. I can't wait for you to show me what you're working with."

As Deon and I were talking, I knew it was time for me to take my birth control pills. So, I decided to reach inside my purse to get them out. For some reason, I couldn't find them. I reached into the backseat to see if I had put the pills in my suitcase. They were not there either. I started to panic, because I knew I couldn't tell Deon that I lost my pills. That's a huge no-no in his book.

"Oh my God, where in the world are those pills? I need an answer, and I need one quick!" As I thought, a light bulb flashed in my head. Oh yeah, now I remember, they are in my make-up bag. I had put my birth control pills in my hand when I had gotten my toothbrush from the bathroom. Thank you, God! I was really panicking. As I was reaching my hand in the backseat, I grabbed for my makeup bag. I began to dump out all of my makeup, and then I pulled my toothbrush out of the bag. For some strange reason, I still didn't find the pills. Now this is just awful! I was beginning to think that when I had gotten my toothbrush, I may have placed the birth control pills back on the bathroom sink. Oh wow! The sad part was that we would be gone for a whole week, and I was going to be without my birth control pills. I hoped nothing would go wrong, because I had been on the pill for about six months and I thought they were in my system long enough not to get pregnant. Even though I had not been taking them correctly, I should still be okay. I had to really ask God to help me to stay focused and not give it away. I just wanted a peaceful week and I refused to let anything go wrong.

Deon looked over at me and said, "Are you okay?"

"Yes, why do you ask?"

"No reason. It just looks like you have something on your mind."

"Oh no, sweetie, I'm okay.

"Well, if you need to talk to me about anything, don't hesitate."

"No, Deon, I'm fine."

As I was sitting in the passenger seat, I felt so awful because I had just lied to my husband. I didn't know what to really say to him, because we rarely argue and being without my birth control pills would definitely bring one up. So as I sat there and enjoyed my ride down interstate 95, I refused to let this bother me.

"Melissa," said Deon.

"Yes, baby," I replied, trying not to sound nervous.

"I will give you hints of where we are going, okay."

"Sure."

"Well, you know that we left Raleigh, North Carolina about four and a half hours ago."

"Yes."

"So now we are heading south."

"Yes, Deon, I can see that." He was talking to me as if I was one of the kids.

"Well, Melissa, we will spend our first night in Savannah, Georgia."

"What is in Savannah?"

"Well, I'm so glad that you asked. Savannah has a lot of history there."

"Wait a minute, Deon. Are you telling me that we are going to spend our anniversary week looking at a historic building?"

"No, Melissa, I just want you and I to take our time and see the world."

"I am sorry. I didn't mean to sound so selfish."

"No problem. I just figured that you are missing the kids, because you haven't been away from them this long."

"I guess that's what it is."

"Deon?"

"Yes, my beautiful queen?"

"You better stop it!" As I leaned over and smiled at him, I said, "Baby, I just want you to know that you don't have to do the things that you do, but I can tell that you love me and I thank you for that."

"Melissa?"

"Yes, my handsome king?"

"I want to thank you also."

"For what, baby?"

"You go way beyond being a wife and a mother. I have taken a lot away from you. And I want to apologize to you."

"No, Deon, you haven't taken anything away from me. I love you very much."

"Melissa, I am so grateful to have you as my wife."

"Well, thank you. I am so grateful to be your wife too. I am so proud to be your wife."

"Girl, you are too funny. You know, Melissa, there has been a lot on my mind."

"Oh yeah. Like what?"

"Well, for an example, you taking birth control pills."

"What!"

"No, not like that. I feel bad because I am making you take those pills and you are my wife."

"Well, Deon, I can understand why you have asked me to do it. So please don't feel bad. Okay?"

"Well, you have been taking them, right?"

"What do you mean, right?"

"I mean, have you been taking them when you are supposed to?"

"Well, do you want to know the truth?"

"Yes I do."

As I turned my head away, I stated, "There have been times when I have forgotten to take them."

"Melissa!"

"Hold on, Deon. When I had realized it, I took two the next day."

"Melissa, do you know you are playing games?"

"No, I am really not trying to play games with you or me. That's why I didn't want to tell you."

"Well, can you do me a favor?"

"What's that, Deon?"

"Can you please make sure you take them on time?"

"Yes, Deon, I will."

"Melissa?"

"Yes."

"When was the last time you took them?"

As I took a deep breath, I replied, "Yesterday."

"Well, if you took them yesterday, then don't you think it's time for you to take them now?"

"Yes, Deon, that is what I am about to do. Thank you for reminding me."

"Well, do you need me to pull over so you can get a cup of water?"

"No, I have a bottle in my bag." I was hoping and praying that Deon would change the subject. Less than a minute later, he started it back up.

"Melissa?"

"Yes, Deon."

"Why haven't I seen you taking your pills yet?"

"Baby, can you please give me a minute?"

"I am sorry. I don't want to keep bothering you about it, but I just don't want us to have any more children."

"Deon, I heard you before."

"I just want to make sure that you understand me."

"I understood you nine months ago. Deon, like I had told you before, birth control pills are not one hundred percent effective."

"You may be right but at least if anything were to happen, I can blame it on the pills and not you."

I tried my best to play it off. I reached inside my purse, hoping that I could find a small piece of candy. I just needed something to place in my mouth so he could just leave me alone and be quiet. I was so happy to have a tiny piece of cracked peppermint at the bottom of my purse. I quickly placed it inside my mouth and sipped on a bottle of water. Thank you, God, because I didn't think he would ever shut up.

We finally arrived in Savannah, Georgia. Everything was just beautiful and so lovely. I never thought that Savannah had so much history. This was definitely a place where Deon and I will bring our children. Later that night, Deon surprised me with a gift. He left it on the bed while he was taking his shower. I figured he wanted me to open it while he was not around. As I open the box, it was some new lingerie. I knew my man had style, but I never thought it was this good.

Once Deon came out of the shower, he had on a brand new pair of silk underwear. "Melissa, do you like it?" Deon asked.

"Yes I do, but don't you think they are fitting you a little tightly?"

"That's the way they are supposed to fit."

"Oh, I didn't know. Well, I'm going to go and take a bath, and I'll be back in a few."

"Okay, baby, take your time. I will be right here."

"I hope so Deon. Especially dressed like that."

While I was in the shower, I was thinking about not having my birth control pills. I was praying that nothing will go wrong while we were on our trip. When I opened the bathroom door, Deon was lying in the bed. He sat up rather quickly, just to see how beautiful I looked. He asked me to turn around so he could get the full view of my lingerie.

"Melissa, baby, you are so sexy and I can't wait to hold and kiss you."

"Well, thank you, Deon," I said. "I can't wait to hold and kiss you either."

That whole night was about Deon and me. We made love the whole entire night.

The next day, Deon had the car packed and we took a journey further down I-95 south. Our next stop was Saint Simons Island, Georgia. I asked Deon what was our purpose for going there.

He replied, "Baby, this island has beautiful water. I would love for us to walk on the beach and then we can go to the lighthouse."

"The light house?" I looked at him as if he was crazy.

"Yes, Melissa, I had always wanted to go and visit Saint Simons Lighthouse."

"Well, when you get there, what are you planning on doing? I hope not walking up the stairs."

"Why not?"

"Why? I just don't like heights!" I exclaimed.

"Aw, Melissa baby, I will not let anything happen to you."

"I know but I rather stay on the ground while you climb it yourself. Because, Lord forgive me, if anything happens to you, someone has to live to tell the story and I guess it will be me."

"Oh, Melissa, don't worry about it. It's like I said before, you are going to be okay, and I want you to walk up the lighthouse stairs with me. Melissa, is it alright with you?"

"No, Deon, it is not alright. But just to hush your mouth, I will do it. Besides, Deon, it sounds like I don't have any other choice."

"Thank you, Melissa."

"You really owe me big, Deon. Oh my gosh, Deon! Look at the water. It is so beautiful. I've never seen such blue water. Baby, is that the lighthouse?"

"Yes it is. Are you ready?"

"No not really, but I will give it a shot."

"How was it, Melissa? Did you enjoy yourself? Tell me the truth; was that so bad, Melissa?"

"Well, Deon, I have to be perfectly honest with you; it wasn't as bad as I thought."

"See, baby, when I tell you to trust me, just go along with it."

"Yeah, whatever."

I really enjoyed my trip to Saint Simons Island. The beach was so beautiful and the lighthouse was fantastic. Deon out-did himself this time. Not to mention the hotel room was wonderful. Deon had surprised me with an ocean-view front room. You could only imagine what happened in there all night.

The next day, we were on our way to our final destination. But Deon still refused to tell me where we were going. It really didn't matter, because if it was like the last two places that we had been, I would be grateful one way or another. I was going to just sit back and enjoy the ride, and I would continue to thank God for blessing me with a great husband.

The closer we got to our destination, Deon had asked for me to close my eyes. I asked him, "Why do I have to close my eyes?" After all, I didn't think it was necessary.

He replied, or should I say yelled, "Because, Melissa, it is a surprise!"

I could feel an argument coming on, so I tried to explain myself. "Well, you know I don't like surprises."

"Please, just do what I ask. Stop being so stubborn."

"Okay, I will close my eyes."

He continued with his surprise. "When I park the car, you can open your eyes."

"This better be a huge surprise, because I just don't understand why I have to go through all of this. Deon?"

"Yes?"

"How long do I have to keep my eyes closed?"

"I really don't want to get smart with you, but could you please just hush and be quiet. You are truly stressing me out. Do you ever listen to yourself talk? I mean, I just asked you one simple thing to do and you are giving me hell. You know what, Melissa?"

"What!"

"Don't worry about it; just keep your eyes open. I am sick and tired of trying to please you. I refuse to keep trying to be the man you want me to be."

"Deon! What are you talking about?"

"Melissa, you know what I am talking about.
I am sick and tired of being sick and tired."

"Deon, where in the world did this come from? We have been having such a wonderful time. I just don't understand."

"Melissa, it came from you!"

"No, Deon, it came from you acting like a butt hole."

"Well, you know what, Melissa, don't worry about the surprise. We are going back home."

"WHAT? Home? How in the world could we just go home when we are almost to our destination?"

"Well, now my destination will be Raleigh, North Carolina."

"How could you do this to me?"

"Melissa, do this to you? What about what you are doing to me?"

"What have I done to you? Tell me if I have done something wrong. Just please forgive me."

"No, Melissa, if you haven't seen what you have been doing wrong, then you are more blind than I thought."

"Wow, Deon, you are so rude."

"I refuse to keep trying to be a good husband to you. For the past three years, I needed my space!"

"Your space? You can never have space as long as we are married and have kids."

"I don't have to be here with you, Melissa."

"I didn't ask you to be with me, but we made a promise before God to stay together."

"Well, I don't know if you had gotten the memo late, but a promise can always be broken."

"Okay, so what are you saying? You don't want to be with me?"

"Melissa, did I say that?"

"Deon, I don't know what you are saying." As Deon was fussing, I reached in the backseat and grabbed my pillow. I just needed to rest my head because I had a long eight-hour ride back to Raleigh, so I might as well close my eyes.

I decided to say a prayer to God, because I really needed someone to talk to. I prayed silently in my mind, "Dear God, this is your girl Melissa. I am here asking you for deliverance. I need your help. Please, God, touch Deon. Please give him a better attitude, and make him love me." As I was praying, tears started to flow from my eyes. I just couldn't believe what I had just gone through. But I knew with the love of God, He will make a way.

Deon's new attitude

Finally, we made it home. I quickly grabbed my bags and went straight into my bedroom. I just needed some space from Deon. Especially, after a long no-talking ride back home. I just didn't want to see or talk to him. As I lay in my bed, Deon decided to come into the bedroom. He had the nerve to ask me if I wanted something to eat. When I turned and looked at him, he knew the answer was no. He quickly said, "Well, if you decide to change your mind, just let me know." I said to myself like heck. I think I will starve before I eat something of his. Lord, where in the world did all of this come from?

As I closed my eyes, I quickly opened them. I remembered my birth control pills were in my bathroom. I jumped up to go get them. I yelled out, "Thank you, God," as I opened the pills. I decided to take the two that I had missed, and four hours later, I would take one more. I thought I should be okay. Someone told me that if I ever forgot to take a birth control pill, the best way for me to get myself back on track, was to take one every four hours until I could get caught back up. So that was just what I did. Lord, I do thank you, because I was so happy that I had finally gotten caught up with all of my pills. I decided to be smart and take Friday's pill on Thursday. I just wanted to make sure I was ahead.

For the past week, Deon and I hadn't talked much. Whenever I was in my bedroom, he was in the living room, watching television or sleeping. I wondered if he felt guilty about what happened the other day. I knew I loved my man, but I just didn't know if he really loved me. Deon had always told me that he would never hurt me and he refused to let anyone else hurt me. I didn't know if mental abuse was a form of hurt to him. As I sat in my bed praying to

God, I asked Him to please strengthen our household. Lord, if there are any spirits in here and it is not of you, then please remove them. I just need some peace all around me. Soon after I finished praying, I fell asleep.

An hour later, I woke up to Deon standing over me. I jumped up, not knowing what he was in here for. He asked, "Is it okay if we could talk?"

I replied, "Talk about what, Deon?"

"If you don't mind, Melissa, would you please sit up? Well, Melissa, I want to start out by saying I really do apologize about the other day. I want to know if you would accept my apology."

"Well, Deon, why are you apologizing about something that you really meant to say?"

"Melissa, how could you tell me that I meant to say something like that?"

"So you are telling me all of the harsh words that you had said, you didn't mean any of them?"

"No, Melissa, I didn't."

"Deon, I want you to know that I do love you, but you have made me feel less than a woman. If I wasn't a child of God, no I wouldn't accept your apology. But being the person who I am, yes I will. Deon, I want you to know one thing."

"What is that, Melissa?"

"I will always forgive, but it will be very hard for me to forget. I just don't know if I could really trust you."

"What is that supposed to mean?"

"Well, Deon, let me say this the correct way. I know that I could probably trust you, but I don't know if you are trustworthy."

"Wow, Melissa, I never thought those words would have ever come out of your mouth!"

"Really, you didn't?"

"No, Melissa, I didn't. I am just surprised that you are acting so difficult."

"Please, don't start with me, Deon! You are standing here and telling me that you are surprised about what I just said to you."

"Yes, Melissa, I am."

"Deon, what about you?"

"Okay, what about me?"

"So you can't recall all the harsh words that you had told me? I have never been like this, Deon. You made me be the person that I am. You did this to me! Each day I have sat in this room, thinking to myself. Not knowing if you are going to pack your clothes and leave me and the kids. I am just so upset right now, but I know I have a God that can change any situation. Deon, how do you think I am feeling right now? For a whole week, I have been having sleepless nights. And I have not eaten much."

"Melissa, why did you just bring this back up again?"

"Deon, what are you talking about? I am letting you know how I'm feeling."

"Well, Melissa, when I first came into this room, I asked you if you accept my apology."

"Okay, I said yes I do."

"So why in the world are you bringing it all back up again?"

"Deon, if you don't know how I am feeling deep down inside, you will never know."

"Well, that may be right, but I just don't want to hear anything else about it."

"Okay, whatever you say."

"Well, Melissa, I have talked to our parents and I told them that we will be on our way to get the kids. Are you ready to go?"

"No, I think it is better for you to go and get them."

"And why are you not going, Melissa? I think it is better for you to go with me."

"For what, Deon? What is the use? I don't want to go around our parents acting as if we are doing so wonderfully. Deon, I am not a fake person. Plus, I think I need to go start dinner."

"Now you want to go and cook?"

"What is that supposed to mean?"

"Heck, Melissa, you haven't cooked in weeks."

"Well, when you said you are going to get my babies, I want to make sure they have something to eat. By the way, Deon, while you are picking up the kids, can you please make sure you give our parents my love?"

"I sure will."

"By the way, Deon, please make sure that you drive safely."

"Yes, Melissa, thank you for being concerned."

"Don't thank me, because that is my job."

Each time that Deon would leave the house, I would always say a special prayer for him, not knowing if he would ever come back home to me. I guess I was just having flashbacks of my father when he last left the house. I might have been angry with my husband, but I didn't want anything bad to happen to him.

"Hey, Melissa?"

"Yes, Deon."

"May I please have a hug?"

"Sure you can."

As Deon was walking out of the house, I still had so much anger built up inside of me, so badly that I just wanted to throw something and hit him upside his head. But I had to remember that I was a praying wife and that would not have been a godly thing to do. Plus, it would be very hard for me to raise my four kids all alone. Thank you, God, for giving me common sense.

Two weeks later, my body was feeling strange. I really believed it was because of those birth control pills. Each day, whenever I would take one, my body would react a little differently. I also had been feeling a little dizzy. But I knew I was guilty, because I had not been taking my pills correctly. But I wanted to at least get them into my system. I thought the best thing for me to do was rest and pray to God that this feeling would just go away.

A week later, I was not feeling any better. I thought I might feel okay if I got a glass of water. Drinking water is usually the best thing for me. As I was standing in the kitchen, Deon had walked up behind me and asked if everything was okay. I turned around and looked at him and said, "Yes, I am okay. I am just feeling a little dizzy, but I will be just fine."

"Melissa, if you are feeling dizzy, you need to just go and sit down."

"No, like I said, I am going to be okay. I just think it is from me taking those birth control pills. But I am really not sure."

"Well, if that is the case, why don't you just make yourself a doctor's appointment?"

"For what, Deon, why should I? Like I said, I am going to be okay. I know what's going on with my body."

"Why in the world do you have to be so rude? All I was trying to do was show some concern."

"I understand that, Deon, but I am okay."

"Well, Melissa, with me being the head of this household, you are going to listen to what I have to say. So you have until tomorrow to make a doctor's appointment and if you don't make yourself one, I will make it for you. Do you understand?"

"Yes, Deon, I understand. But why are you talking to me like I am one of the kids?"

"Well, Melissa, at times you act like one."

"Instead of me arguing with you, I think it will be best for me to just walk away."

"Well, Melissa, do whatever you have to do."

Lord, I really don't know why I put up with his mess.

So later on that day, I decided to make myself a doctor's appointment just to hush up Deon's mouth. I was told that I could come in the next day at nine-thirty in the morning. Thank goodness Deon was off, because I didn't want to take all of my kids to my appointment.

The doctor visit

As I was in the room talking to Doctor Jerome and Nurse Miwon, I told them exactly what was going on with me. I was embarrassed to tell them about me not taking my birth control pills correctly. But I had to be truthful. As I was talking, Doctor Jerome quickly asked me to stop.

He said, "Hold on, Melissa. I wanted to make sure I heard you right. Did you say that you have not been taking your pills?"

"Yes sir. I have tried so hard to take them on time, but it is so difficult."

"Well, Melissa, do you know that not taking your pills correctly could cause you to get pregnant?"

"Yes sir, I heard. But I don't think I am."

"Why don't you think you are pregnant?

"I have been taking my pills twice a day."

"What! Are you crazy, Melissa?"

"Doctor Jerome!"

"Sorry Melissa, I didn't mean it like that. But you can cause danger to your body if you take the pills incorrectly."

"I didn't know that. Well, I guess I do now."

"Okay, Melissa, here is what we can do. I don't have any choice but to give you a pregnancy test. And if it comes back negative, I will give you an insert."

"An insert?"

"Yes Melissa, an insert is something that I could insert into your vagina."

"My vagina!"

"Yes, but it is no harm to your body. It's just another form of birth control."

"Doctor Jerome, I really don't know about that."

"Okay Melissa, if you can promise me that you can take the birth control pills on time, then I will allow you to continue to use them. But before we go any further, I will need for you to take a pregnancy test."

"Oh, Doctor Jerome, I really don't want to take it."

"Well, Melissa, you really don't have a choice."

"I know, but I am so scared."

"Well, the promising thing about it is, you are married."

"That might be true, but my husband told me that he doesn't want any more children. As a matter of fact, Deon had wanted to get a vasectomy."

"Well, what was wrong with that?"

"I didn't feel comfortable with my husband getting that done."

"Do you have a reason why you don't feel comfortable?"

"No sir, I really don't." After a long pause, I decided to tell the truth. "Well, I kind of do."

"Okay what is it?"

I began my long drawn-out explanation. "Well, when I was younger, I watched a movie, and in the movie was a husband and his wife. He was the type of husband who would cheat on his wife every chance that he would get. But before he started cheating on his wife, he talked her into letting him get a vasectomy. I always told myself that whenever I got married, I would never let my husband do that to himself."

"Melissa, you shouldn't base your marriage on a movie."

"I know I shouldn't, but I wanted to be on the safe side."

"Let me ask you a question."

"Yes sir."

"Hold on, do me a favor first. Go to the restroom and pee in this cup."

After I finished peeing in the cup, I came back into the room. Doctor Jerome was waiting on me.

"Okay, Melissa, it shouldn't take long for your results. Now back to our discussion. I want to ask you a personal question. Do you trust your husband?"

"Yes, I think I do," I said in a puzzling voice. "Why do you ask?"

"Because whenever we talk on certain subjects, you seem to be a little scared. So I just wanted to make sure everything is okay."

"Oh yes, Doctor Jerome, I am fine and we both are doing just fine. Deon is a great man. I love him and I know for a fact that he loves me."

"Well, that sounds better. I was really beginning to worry about you two."

As the door opened, Nurse Miwon walked in with my results in hand. I really became nervous, but I knew there was no way that I was pregnant.

"Hi, Melissa."

"Hi again, Nurse Miwon."

"There is no easy way to tell you this, but you are pregnant."

"PREGNANT!" I knew everyone in the waiting room heard me scream. "Hold on, Nurse Miwon, did the word 'pregnant' just come out of your mouth? Please tell me that you are just playing. Please. Lord, I just can't be pregnant." I wanted her to tell me differently, but that was not going to happen. I was so disappointed that tears were flowing from my eyes. There was no way that I could tell Deon. Through my tears, I managed to say, "Doctor Jerome, I don't know what I am going to do."

He was puzzled by my statement but still gave me words of encouragement.

"You will do exactly what you have always done."

"No, you don't understand."

"Tell me then, Melissa."

"See, Deon and I said we will not have any more kids."

"Oh, is that something that you two said?"

"Well, not exactly. Deon was the one who originally said it."

"I thought so."

"Why did you ask?"

"Because I know you better than you think. Melissa, can you recall back when you had your first child?"

"Yes."

"Do you remember telling me that God is always with you, even in the midst of your storm?"

"Yes I do. But that was about four years ago."

"Do you still feel the same way?"

"A little."

"Well, what changed your mind?"

"Deon."

"I don't understand."

"Well, Doctor Jerome, he is going to be very upset with me. I don't know what I am going to do."

"Well, Melissa, didn't you tell me that you and him are doing just fine?"

"Yes sir, I did."

"And if that is the case, he should be okay. Right?"

"No, Doctor Jerome, I was not totally honest with you. Actually, Deon and I haven't been doing well at all. At least for the last month, we haven't. We tried to work things out, but the more he and I would talk, the more we would argue."

"Well, Melissa, that is a part of marriage. Plus, you don't have a choice but to tell your husband. If you want me to, I will do it for you."

"No thank you, I will do it. I don't know how, but I will."

Nurse Miwon could sense how I was feeling and stated, "Melissa, if you ever feel that you need to talk, I am here."

"Thank you so much."

"You are welcome. Melissa, do you still have my phone number?"

"Yes, I do." I turned around with a sad look on my face then gathered my belongings. "Okay, now I have to go home and face the music. Thank you, but honestly no thanks."

"Well, we are very sorry, Melissa."

"No, please, Doctor Jerome, don't apologize. You were just

doing your job."

"I know, Melissa, but I will be seeing you soon."

"Okay."

As I was driving home, I was trying to rehearse the words that I needed to say to Deon. I was just hoping that he would be okay. I was so scared for my life, because I was so sick and tired of arguing with him. Now my pregnancy was only going to add fuel to the fire. Lord, please give me the right words to say.

Finally, I arrived home. As I walked into the house, my kids were jumping, yelling and screaming, "Mommy, we missed you."

I replied, "Mommy missed you too."

Catherine asked, "Mommy, did you bring me something back from the store?"

"No baby, I didn't go to the store." If my baby only knew. I may not have brought her anything from the store, but I did bring her something back. As I was in the kitchen getting myself a glass of water, Deon walked in.

"Hey, baby, how did your doctor's visit go?"

I was so nervous, because I just didn't know what to say. I replied, "It went well." Then I decided that I would have to tell him something about the visit. So I blurted out, "Oh yeah, I was told that I needed to stay off the pills for a while."

"And why is that?" he replied.

"Well, Deon, those birth control pills are too strong for my body. That's what I was told."

"So if that is the case, Melissa, what will you be using for birth control?"

"Doctor Jerome told me to use condoms for now."

"Condoms!"

"Yes, honey, it will be only for a little while. Just until the new birth control pills come out."

"What new pills?"

"They are making some that are not too strong for females."

Deon gave me a look of uncertainty. "I never heard of that."

"Deon, that's what I was told."

"Melissa, we just have to do what we have to do."

"Yes I know. Well, I need to go to the restroom."

"Okay, Melissa," he said, as if he totally believed me. I was truly relieved.

As I was using the restroom, I felt so guilty, because I had just lied to Deon. I didn't know what to tell him. I was just so scared to tell him the truth. I knew that I would have to tell him sooner or later, but right now, this was not the time. Lord, please give me strength and help me to get through this storm. Please! As I was talking to God, there was a knock on the door. It was Deon.

"Melissa, are you okay?" he yelled.

"Yes I am."

"Well, who are you talking to?"

"No one, I was just singing a song."

"Well, dinner is almost done. Are you ready to eat?"

"Yes, just give me a few minutes and I will be there."

"Okay, baby, I will just go ahead and have your plate fixed."

"Thanks, Deon, that sounds good." Oh my God, now that was close. I had to stay in the bathroom an extra minute to regroup.

As I was at the dinner table, Deon asked me if I was okay. I simply nodded my head. He gave me a strange look and said, "Well, since you have been back, you seem to have a lot on your mind."

All I could say was, "No, I am okay. Just tired, I guess. I think I'm going to lie down for about an hour or two."

"Melissa, I am going to clean up and wash up the kids. Just go and get you some rest, and if you need me, I will be here."

"Thank you, and by the way, thanks for dinner. It was great."

"You are welcome. Now go and get you some rest." He was being the dear, sweet husband I used to know.

As I was lying in my bed, I reached over to get the house phone. I needed to talk to someone. So I decided to call my mother. I was so relieved when she answered the phone. "Hi Mother, how are you doing?"

"I am doing just fine. I missed seeing you the other day, Melissa."

"I miss you also, Mother."

"So is everything going okay?"

"Yes, as well as to be expected," I said.

"What is that supposed to mean?" she replied.

As I took a deep breath, I began to explain. "Mama, Deon and I haven't been doing too good."

"Wow, Melissa, I didn't know that. So tell me what is going on."

"It started back on our anniversary trip. The first two days went by well. But on the third day-." She could sense the hesitation in my voice.

"Melissa, what happened on third day?" she exclaimed.

"Mama, Deon was kind of difficult."

"Tell me about it, honey."

"When Deon and I had gotten to our final destination, he wanted me to close my eyes."

"What's wrong with that?"

"I told him that I really don't like surprises. Now, Mother, you know I don't."

"Yes, I remember that about you."

"We had argued for a while until Deon just said to forget it and turned around, and we headed back home."

"Wow, really. So you telling me that you and Deon were almost to your destination and an argument occurred?" I could hear disbelief in her voice. "And from that argument, he turned around and drove all the way back home?"

"Yes, that is what I'm saying." I knew she was on my side. "Now tell me he was wrong for that."

"Well, Melissa, yes he was very wrong, but you were also wrong." There was a long pause; she knew I didn't understand. "Well, Melissa, in a marriage, there is give and take." She began to explain it in a way that only a mother could. "You were being a little stubborn. You have to learn not to take everything literally." She continued on, "You have to give a little too, okay." Then she put her shout voice on. "I am very disappointed in the both of you, but I guess this is a lesson learned."

I hesitantly agreed. "Yes, now that you explained it, you are right. We both were wrong."

"Well, Melissa, I am not going to point fingers, but you have to be careful. Deon was trying to make you happy. I think, overall, he is a good man. Am I right?" She knew she was right without me answering. I guess she just wanted me to confess that I knew I had a good man. "Now is there anything else you need to tell me?"

I figured I might as well tell her. "Yes, as a matter of fact, there is. Really, there is no better way to say it: I am pregnant."

"WHAT!" I held the phone back because I knew that was coming.

"Yes, that's what I said."

"Okay, so what did Deon say?"

"Hmm, he didn't say anything, because he doesn't know yet." "Why not?" She yelled at me again.

"Because Deon and I had talked before and he told me that he doesn't want any more kids. At first, he wanted to go and get a vasectomy and I was totally against it." I gave her the same story that I gave Doctor Jerome. "Mother, I just don't feel comfortable about my husband getting that done. I don't have a reason," I pleaded.

"Really, Melissa, you do have a reason."

"Mother, I think you know me better than I know myself." So I gave up the same answer as before. "I just feel if a man would get that done, it is a better chance that he would go out and cheat."

"Melissa, I want you to understand something." I could tell that her finger was up and going back and forth as if I was there with her. "If a man wants to cheat, they don't need a vasectomy." She continued preaching, "They will just do it."

I interrupted her, "True. But I don't know." I was just frustrated that she didn't understand.

"Well, so what are you going to do, now that you're pregnant?"

"I don't know."

"How far along are you?"

"You know what? I never asked." I didn't think to ask; I was so shocked.

"Well, I am going to be in your area tomorrow; if you can call the doctor's office for an appointment, I will go with you."

"Mother, you will?" I was so happy for her support.

"Yes, Melissa, I want you to always remember that you are always going to be my daughter. And whatever you go through, good or bad, I will always be here." Her voice was so calm and reassuring. "I want you to know that I will always love you and will you please remember one thing?"

"What's that?"

"That God is in control."

"Mother?"

"Yes, baby?"

"Thank you."

"No problem, I will see you tomorrow. Now get off the phone and call your doctor." She managed to throw that in before she hung up.

The next day, I was given a 9:30 doctor's appointment. I was very happy that Deon went to work that day, so I didn't have to explain to him where I had to go. Since my mother was at the doctor's office with me, she was able to sit with the children in the waiting room. As I came out into the lobby to tell my mother the news, Catherine was staring at me. I knew that I couldn't tell my mother anything with her around. Catherine was such a daddy's girl, and if she were to hear me say anything about being pregnant, she would definitely tell Deon. So I had to wait until we had gotten the kids into the car.

"Okay, Melissa, what did they say?"

"I am two-and-a-half months pregnant."

"Wow, two-and-a-half months, so you really don't have a choice but to tell him."

"Doctor Jerome was very surprised, because after he found out about how far I was, he decided to make sure the baby was okay."

"Melissa, what made him decide to do that?"

"Well, with me taking birth control pills, he just wanted to make sure I have not done any harm to my baby."

"Well, I could understand that. So what did he find out?"

"Everything looks good so far."

"Great, but do you need for me to be there when you tell Deon?"

"No, I will do it later." I didn't want my mother to hear us argue.

"Melissa, you really need to do it now." She was so concerned.

I took a deep breath and responded, saying, "Yes I know, Mama. I want to thank you for coming and being by my side." She knew there was no changing my mind. "I am going to head home and prepare dinner for the kids and Deon."

"Okay Melissa, I love you and don't forget to call me later." I nodded and watched as she departed.

An outrageous conversation

Later that evening, we were at the table eating dinner. I asked Deon, how was his day. I was just trying to warm up to the idea of telling him, but I just couldn't. I was sitting there thinking to myself, saying, "If he only knew." Trying to stay busy, I offered to clean the kitchen and put up the food. Deon insisted on helping me, but I didn't want him to sense that something was wrong. I finally convinced him to help the children instead, so he got the children ready for bed. I was truly relieved; it gave me a moment to myself. As I was finished with the kitchen, Deon asked me to come into the living room so we could watch a movie together. I really didn't want to, because I had so much on my mind. I knew sitting there and watching the movie with him would only make things worse. All I could do was think about what my mother said to me about relationships: "Make sure you learn how to be a giver not a taker." So, I decided to sit and watch the movie.

As the movie ended, I asked Deon if he didn't mind if we talked. As I gathered my nerves, I stated, "Well, I don't know where to start." Then I just sat there looking down.

"Just say it, Melissa," he said, as he placed his hand on my shoulder.

"Well, Deon, I wished that it was that easy." I knew he was truly puzzled.

Frightened, he whispered, "What's wrong, baby? You can tell me."

As I took a deep breath, I just told him. "I found out that I am pregnant."

"What!!!" he shouted. "I know like hell you just didn't tell me that you are pregnant!" Deon grabbed me by my arms and said, "Melissa, tell me that you are lying to me."

I shook my head. "I'm not lying. I am really pregnant." As the tears were rolling down my face, I began to apologize, "I'm so sorry for -." I couldn't finish.

"For what, Melissa?" he demanded. "If anyone is sorry, it's me." He continued shouting, "I knew that I should not have depended on you." As he stood over me, I could see the anger in his eyes. Deon continued shouting, "I should have gone ahead and got that vasectomy done, so it is not your fault. It's mine! I trusted that you could do what was right." After he calmed down, he sat back down and asked, "So how far along are you, because you already know that we are not having any more children. You already know that, right?"

"No, Deon, I don't," I replied. "I am not going to sit here and listen to you," I shouted, "but to answer your question, I am two-and-a-half months pregnant!"

"How in the world could you be two-and-a-half months pregnant when you were on birth control pills?"

"Deon, that's what I said to the doctor."

"Knowing the type of person you are, Melissa, you probably didn't take your pills on time." He spoke to me as if I was a child.

"How in the world could you say that?" I asked in disbelief. "I did!"

In his condescending voice, he said, "Well, if you did, you shouldn't be pregnant." He continued, "Like I said, we are not having any more children, so I think the best thing for you to do is have an abortion."

I knew my ears were deceiving me. "A what?"

"Yes, you heard me, an ABORTION!" He did not budge from the idea. "I am not playing with you. I am dead serious."

"Deon, did you hear how far along I am?"

"Yes, I did."

"So there is no way that I could do that," I tried to explain.

"And why not, Melissa?"

"Common sense, Deon," I finished my explanation. "If I were

to get an abortion, it won't just kill our baby, it could also kill me."

"Well, Melissa, that's a chance that we just have to take."

"Deon, how could you say that?"

"You know what, Melissa, you are right." I thought that he had finally come to his senses, but he didn't. "Once the baby is born, I want you to give it up for adoption."

I just cried, "Deon, I am not going to do that either. I will not!"

"Why, Melissa?" he demanded. "Tell me why!"

"Think about it, Deon." I tried to show him the error of his ways. "Together, we have four kids."

"That's right," he interrupted. "Melissa, that's all that we need."

"But I refuse to give away something that came from us," I pleaded with him. "I just won't do it!"

"Well, Melissa, if you don't do it, I am not going to be the good husband that I promised I would be."

"So what are you saying to me?"

"I will show you better than I can tell you," he stated, as he angrily walked out of the living room. Deon grabbed his car keys and left the house without a word. What a terrible nightmare this has been. Deon stayed out all night and he didn't come home until the next evening. That was unlike him. I didn't know what I should do. I wondered if I needed to call the police or try and find him myself. It was a very stressful day being home without my husband. I decided to call my mother to let her know what was going on with Deon and me. I needed someone to talk to, and with her being my mother, there was no one else better. As my mother and I were talking, she told me to make sure that I pray, because Deon was just upset and he just needed a minute to himself.

"A minute?" I said. "Mother, Deon has been gone since last night. I feel there is nothing good out in the streets late at night."

"All I can do is tell you to focus on God, and He will direct your path."

"Thank you so much, Mother. I will give him some time to think."

"That is all you can do at this point."

"You are right." To tell you the truth, she's always right.

"I will talk to you later."

"Thank you so much, Mother."

Later that day, Deon came into the house and didn't say a word to me. He played with the kids and made sure they were doing okay. I asked him if he was hungry and he didn't respond until Catherine said, "Daddy, did you hear Mama talking to you?"

He shook his head and pretended as if he didn't hear me, then said, "What did you say, Melissa?"

"Well, I asked if you were hungry because I cooked your favorite meal."

Much to my surprise, he said, "No, I already ate."

So I asked, "Would you like to talk later?"

"No, Melissa," he stressed. "I think we did a lot of talking last night."

As bad as I wanted to yell at him, a flashbulb came into my head. I remembered what my mother had told me that I needed to give him some space. When he decides that he is ready to talk, then he will come to me. I just wasn't thinking.

Each day that went by, we were still not talking. Deon stayed out of the house more than ever. He made sure the kids saw him enough. As soon as they were asleep, he was gone. This was the hardest pregnancy that I ever had to deal with. If it wasn't for my mother, I just don't know what I would have done.

I did tell Deon's mother about my pregnancy, and she didn't seem very happy. So I decided not to talk much to her. I think Deon had gotten to her before I did. Like any other mother would do, she would make sure that she supported her son in everything he did.

I was in the last month of my pregnancy. I wasn't sure if Deon was going to be there for the birth or not. However, I knew one thing was for sure: my mother, Robert Junior, and my best friend Jessica would definitely be there. Still, there is nothing like having Deon by my side.

Kimberly

It was April 22, and I was scheduled to give birth to our baby. I was very excited, but at the same time, I was saddened, because Deon still hadn't given me his answer. I was really hoping and praying that he would be there. But only God could change his heart.

As I was in my room at the hospital, getting ready for the birth of our baby, Deon was still not here. My mother whispered in my ear and assured me that Deon would be here. Still, I wasn't sure because he never told me. I had to believe my mother; she never lied to me before and she wouldn't start now. While I was getting prepped for the birth, surprisingly Deon walked into the room. I was shocked! My mother hadn't lied. But no one knew what I had been going through for the past nine months with Deon. This was a battle that I don't wish for anyone.

When he walked into the room, he gave me a hug and a kiss on my cheek. As he smiled, he also whispered into my ear and said, "Melissa, I am not here for you. I just didn't want to look as if I am a deadbeat dad." He continued whispering, "I don't want your mother to think badly of me."

I looked up at Deon with daggers in my eyes and said, "How could you come into my room and tell me this? You really wasted your time coming here." I pointed to the door. "Deon, if you don't mind, I would like for you to leave."

Our whispering match continued as he reached for my hand. "Melissa, there is no way that I am going to do that."

I looked over to my mother, only to see her in a corner reading a book. I was very thankful that she didn't hear anything we were talking about. With a fake smile pasted on my face, I replied, "Well,

Deon, I really don't want you here."

He grinned and said, "Melissa, sorry but this time, it is not what you want."

"Whatever!"

With all the arguing, I began to go into labor. I took a deep breath. As I began to push, Deon was rubbing my head. He told me to take my time and push and everything was going to be okay. The more he talked, the worse I was feeling. I never wanted to live my life like this, especially with my husband. It was bad enough that he didn't live at the house half of the time. I didn't know what to think. It was very hard for me to think about it. The more I thought about it, the more sick I got. I never hoped for a marriage like this.

"Push!" my mother was yelling. "I can see the baby."

"I am pushing," I replied.

Finally, I had my baby.

"It's a girl!" said Doctor Jerome. "You have yourself another girl."

"Aw, she is so beautiful." said my mother. Then she turned to Deon, "You and Melissa have done a wonderful job."

With a smile, he said, "Thank you, but I really owe it all to Melissa."

"So Melissa, what are you going to name her?" my mother asked.

Without looking at Deon, I just said, "Well, I was thinking of the name Kimberly."

"Kimberly," mother said with a smile on her face. "That's a nice name. I really like that."

"Thank you, Mother." Then I looked over to Deon and I asked him, "How do you feel about Kimberly?"

"I think Kimberly is a nice name," he replied with a twisted look on his face. "It really doesn't matter to me."

Fishing for his true sense of feeling, I stressed, "So what do you think about her, Deon?"

He smiled. "I think she is a beautiful baby. I really think we have done a great job together." He turned to my mother and excused himself. "I am going, because I have to get back to work."

I shouted, "Work! Why are you going to work at a time like this?"

"Melissa, think about it. Someone has to make the money." He looked at me. "We now have five children, and if I don't work, no one will."

Upset and almost crying, I asked, "So what time are you getting off?"

"I don't know."

"I may be going home tomorrow. Will you be here to pick me up?"

"Just call and let me know what time you are leaving, okay."

"I will. Deon, I love you."

"Okay, see you later, Melissa."

As I watched him leave the room, I cried. I knew my marriage was turning for the worse. I was very happy for the love and the support of my mother.

"Melissa," she said, "I want you to understand one thing."

"What's that, Mother?"

"I want you to keep your head up and don't you ever let a man know that he is tearing you down."

"Yes, ma'am, I know, but it is so hard."

"I know it can be, but just remember what I have told you."

"Well, I am now stuck raising five kids."

"You are not stuck. This is something that you have chosen to do. I respect you tremendously for that. Some women would have done the opposite. You are strong in your faith, Melissa. I love you for listening to the spirit and not your husband. I can only imagine what he suggested you do when you told him that you were pregnant. You never know, Kimberly could be the chosen one. So thank you, baby, for honoring God. I knew, deep in my heart, I had raised you right."

"Mother, yes you have. I really love you. I guess, deep in my heart, I am hurting, because if my father was here, I would not be going through this."

"You may be right, but I know one thing for sure."

"What's that?"

"He is here. You will be surprised how much he is seeing. So just stay prayed-up and keep believing in God."

"Yes I will. Mother, I want to thank you."

"For what?"

"I remember I used to complain about going to church three times a week."

"Well, Melissa, I can understand. You were young and there were other things that you had wanted to do."

"Yes, but you stood your ground, and made sure we went to church. I am so happy that you had made that choice. It is very hard for me to get Deon to go."

"Melissa, think about it. Deon wasn't raised much in the church. Especially after his mother had gotten severely abused."

"Well, don't you think that should have been the perfect time for her to go?"

"No, Melissa. You have to think about it. Sometimes, church folks are worse than just regular folks."

"Mother, why would you say that?"

"At times, they act like they care, but at the same time, they are talking about you."

"True."

"Some judgmental church folks can be harsh. So when she was abused, she didn't want to go around some of the church people. She didn't want her business around the town."

"I could understand that."

"His dad had been messing around on his mom for years. She had to deal with a lot. She said it was very hard trying to raise Deon and work two jobs."

"I didn't think about it like that."

"Yes baby, it's a sad situation."

"Well, Mother, I just wish that Deon would think about how going to church would be a good thing for the kids to see him do."

"If he hasn't yet, he will. Just give him some time."

"Time! I think that's all I have been giving him, especially for the past nine months." She just didn't understand. "Well, I just hope it won't be too late."

"Melissa, just pray. Like I always told you, if you just take a moment out of your day and pray, baby, it can change any situation.

"Yes, ma'am, I will." I was so thankful that Robert Jr. and Jessica were in the lobby watching the kids, so they didn't have a clue of what was going on with Deon and me.

"Melissa?"

"Yes."

"Why don't you try and rest, while I watch Kimberly?"

"That sounds great."

"Mother?"

"Yes, Melissa."

"Thank you so much, for all of your encouraging words. I just don't know what I would ever do without you. I love you with all of my heart."

"Baby, you know that I love you too. Now give your mother a hug." As I was hugging my mother, I couldn't let her go. I really needed that hug. The more that I held on to my mother, the harder I cried. The amazing thing was, we both cried together. How blessed that I am to have such a wonderful mother.

The next day, I was so excited, because Kimberly and I were able to go home. I was all packed and ready to leave, but there was one problem: Deon had not arrived yet. I was thankful to have my mother there with me, but there would have been nothing like having my Deon.

Finally, it was time for me to check out. I talked to him about an hour ago, and he told me that he was on his way. I prayed that he was coming. Two hours later, Deon finally arrived. I was a little upset, especially only living twenty minutes from the hospital. But I didn't want my frustration to show in front of my mother. I just wanted to get home.

While in the room, I asked Deon, "Will you please hold Kimberly while I get my stuff together?"

He turned towards me and said, "I think it's best if you hold her because my hands are dirty."

I had never heard of such a thing. There was a sink in the room where he could have washed his hands. So there wasn't any excuse. All I could do was pray to God that I would not have any problems with him. I just wanted a happy and loving marriage. I refused to live like that. I was so glad that my mother decided to come home with me. She knew that Deon was working a lot of hours, and felt that it was best for her to spend at least a week with me and the kids. I really felt in my heart that my mother knew more than she was saying. I was very happy, because I really didn't want to be home alone with Deon and the kids, especially with the attitude that he was having.

Changes

A few years later, my marriage had gotten worse. Deon decided that he only wanted to work the night shift. I was very upset, because I had to stay up all night with Kimberly and the rest of the kids. Deon became very stingy with his money. He claimed that the money that he makes is only enough to pay the bills and put groceries in the house. I just didn't understand. I had to do a lot of thinking and I came up with the conclusion that I needed to get a job. I remembered that wanting a job was something that Deon didn't want to hear. One day, I brought up the subject again. I took a deep breath and I confronted Deon with my idea. "Deon," I said, "I feel that it is in our best interest for me to get a job."

"Well, Melissa, I also was doing a lot of thinking." Oh Lord, I said to myself. When Deon thinks, there is no telling what's on his mind, or what will come out of his mouth. He replied, "I also feel that it is in your best interest to get a job. I am tired of being the only one working around here. I feel like I am being used."

"Hold on, Deon." I stopped him dead in his tracks. "I have not been using you at all! If anything, I have been a very supportive wife to you. I refuse to let you say that I have been using you. I am a damn good woman. If any one of us has been used, Deon, it is me!"

"Hold on, Melissa, how in the world could you say that I have been using you? As long as we have been married, I have been the only one working."

"Deon, don't go there, because I had offered to get a job."

"I don't want to hear your lies."

"Deon, I am tired."

"Well, Melissa, I am tired too."

"What are you tired of? I know that our kids deserve more than this. I won't settle for less."

"Melissa, I will make a deal with you."

"What's that?"

"Okay, as long as I am working the night shift, you can work as many jobs as you like."

"As many jobs as I like?"

"Yes, that's what I'm saying."

"Deon, I don't have any comments."

"Well, you shouldn't."

"You know what, Deon?"

"What?"

"I do have a question for you."

"What's that, Melissa?"

"When can I have my husband back?"

"What are you talking about?"

"Deon, you know what I am talking about. I'm sick and tired of you not being home with me and our kids. Sometimes, at night, our son Leon would get up, and ask for his father. I know that you don't work every night of the week."

"Well, Melissa, I may not work every night, but I work enough."

"So you are telling me that you rather stay out in the streets with who knows what, than be home with your wife and kids?"

"No, I'm not saying that."

"So what are you saying because I really need to know?"

"Melissa, I don't have to explain anything to you."

"I don't know where you had gotten that from, because the last I checked, we are still married."

"Melissa, don't remind me."

"Stop being so hateful ,Deon."

"Please! I am not being hateful. I am just drained."

"Deon?"

"What, Melissa?"

"Do you remember the first time I met your mother?"

"Yes, I do remember."

"Then afterward, I asked you about meeting your father."

"Okay, Melissa, so what does that have to do with us?"

"Don't you remember telling me that you never wanted to live like that?"

"Yes, I do remember telling you that. So what are you saying, Melissa?"

"I don't see the same man that I met or married. And I don't see the same man who used to tell me that he loved me every day. Where in the world is my husband?"

"I don't know, Melissa. I think you better go and look for him."

"Please, Deon, if you can find him, please send him home to his wife and kids."

"Melissa, I don't know where he is."

"Okay, Deon, I will just continue to pray for him then."

"That might be the best thing that you can do. Just pray."

"Oh I will! Deon?"

"What, Melissa?"

"Do you mind if I pray for us now?"

"Do whatever you want to."

"No, I want you and me to hold hands and pray."

"Well not now, Melissa."

"Why not?"

"I have to go and get ready for work."

"No problem, I will pray anyway."

"You just do that."

"Is that all you can say, Deon? How inconsiderate are you! I know that you were raised better than that."

"Don't sit here and talk about how I was raised!"

"Well, Deon, where is the love?"

"What love? It went out the window three years ago."

"I am not going to stand here any longer and argue with you."

"Please, Melissa, don't."

As I walked into my room, I just got down on my knees and

cried out to God. I felt in my heart that Deon was possessed with an evil spirit. I knew my husband better than that. All I could do was just continue to pray for him.

My first job

After searching for about a week, I was blessed with my first job. I was so happy, because I had a job as a server. I didn't know the first thing about being a server, but I knew that my kids had needs. Every day, whenever I would come home, Deon would always ask me how much money I made. That was really beginning to get on my nerves, because he did not first ask me how my day had gone. All he wanted was for me to pay some of the bills. So the best thing for me to do was lie. I told Deon that I only made thirty dollars, when I really made sixty. I knew with the job that he had, he could afford to pay all the bills in the house. I am not crazy. He had been doing it all along. So what's the problem now? I really didn't trust him, especially when he didn't come home at a decent time. I refused to be dumb. All I could do was continue to pray and ask God for a changed man.

Kimberly speaks out

Another year had gone by, and each day, I would come home from work, Kimberly would always run to me crying. I never knew what was wrong with her. I just figured that she just missed her mother. Until one day, she and I went to the grocery store. Kimberly asked me if it was all right if we could talk. With my baby only being three and a half years old, I was excited to hear what she had to say. "Mama," Kimberly said, "well whenever you go to work my brothers and sisters are mean to me."

"They are?" I asked.

"Yes, ma'am." She was so serious.

"How are they mean to you, Kimberly?"

"Well, whenever they get into trouble, they blame it on me."

"Oh they do?"

"Yes, mama."

"Like how, Kimberly?"

"Mother, please don't say anything to daddy."

"Why not?"

"Well, because he doesn't believe anything I say."

I thought to myself that my baby probably knows what she is saying. I know how her daddy can be towards her. I just wished that he wouldn't show it.

"Well, Kimberly, I need to talk to someone."

"No, Mama, please!"

"Fine, I won't do it."

"Well, Mama, they were playing in the kitchen and broke a plate. Daddy asked who did it, and they blamed it on me."

"What did your daddy do?"

"He told us all to come into the living room and that's when he beat us. I was mad because I wasn't in there at all. The worst part, Mama, was - ."

I interrupted her before she could get it out, "What, baby? Tell me."

"Well, when Daddy beat the other four, he didn't beat them long at all, but when it was my turn, he kept beating me for a very long time. I kept crying and crying, but he just wouldn't stop."

"Kimberly, my poor baby." I was almost in tears when she told me that.

"I am so sorry. Mother, I don't want you to tell anyone because when you go to work they will get me."

"I don't know what to do. I don't want you to have to suffer when I'm not there."

"Well, Mama, I am going to be okay."

All she wanted was to keep me happy. Lord, please have mercy on my baby. Please protect her from all hurt, harm, and danger. I don't know what else to do. Lord, if it is your will, please give my husband and kids a change of heart when it comes to Kimberly. I feel, deep in my heart, that Deon allows a lot of bad things to happen to Kimberly. I understand that he didn't really want her, but please, Lord, he doesn't need to show our kids that he feels that way.

"Well, Kimberly, I will make sure I do whatever I need to do. Even if it is letting Jessica keep you while I am at work."

"No, Mother."

"Okay. Kimberly?"

"Yes."

"Thank you so much for letting me know what was going on in the house."

"I love you so much, Mama."

"I love you too."

Kimberly would be turning four in a month; I fully prayed that things would get better.

"Mother?"

"Yes, Kimberly."

"Does Daddy love me?"

"Yes, your daddy loves you. Why do you think he doesn't?"

"Well, he gives the other ones hugs and kisses and he just fuss at me."

"I don't know why, baby. But I do know he loves you."

I was saying to myself, "My baby knows more than she thinks. I just can't sit here and tell her the truth about her father. I refuse to."

"Well, Kimberly, would you like to cook dinner with me tonight?"

"For real, Mama!"

"Yes, baby, I am for real."

Her little face lit up when she said, "Thank you, Mama, thank you."

"You are welcome."

Kimberly started chanting, "I love you, Mama. I love you, Mama. There is no other like my mother. I love you, Mama!"

"I love you too, Kimberly." Deep in my heart, I was hurting, because my baby was so sweet and she didn't deserve any of this. She would always know that her mother always loved her. I didn't regret one day about having her. If I had to go through this all over again, I would.

Kimberly's party

A month later, it was Kimberly's fourth birthday. I had planned a big party for my baby. With my mother, Robert Jr., Jessica and with Deon's mother and father coming, I knew she was going to have a good time. I was happy that Deon's mother and I were able to talk again, because she and I hadn't talked in about two years. It bothered me at first, but I had to learn to get over it. I guess without her seeing her grand-kids on a regular basis, it bothered her too. She called and said that she felt very guilty about not being here for her grand-kids. So she wanted to make things up, by helping me with Kimberly's birthday party. At first, I wanted to tell her no, and that I already had it taken care of, but I had to think for a second. Realizing that her son barely did anything around here, I would be the dummy not to accept her help.

Once my mother came over, I was in my room getting dressed. She knocked on the door to ask if I needed any help for the party. I told her no, that I had everything taken care of, but I thanked her anyway.

"Mother, can you believe that Deon's mother is paying for most of Kimberly's party?"

"No I can't. What made her come around and step up?"

"I don't know. She just called one day and apologized to me."

"What was her excuse?"

"She never gave me one. She just wanted to see her grand-kids, so she said."

"Now, Melissa, don't feel like that. You know she is a good person. You never know what Deon could have told her."

"Mother, you may be right, but that is no excuse for her actions."

"Well, honey, just thank God that He has given her a change of heart."

"Yes, Mother, I already have."

As I began to giggle, my mother asked, "What's so funny?"

"I know I may be wrong, but I still have a stash of money that I saved from my job that I refuse to tell Deon about. I could have paid for Kimberly's birthday party myself, but I didn't have to."

"Melissa, like I have always said, don't you forget that you have money in your private bank account."

"Yes I remember."

"Have you told Deon yet?"

"No and I don't have any intentions of telling him. Why should I? He doesn't deserve to know anything. Well at least not now. I want to make sure Deon gets some help first. Mother, did I tell you that Deon still doesn't come home at night?"

"No, Melissa, you didn't tell me that."

"He stays out all night, but the last I checked, he only works until 3:30 in the morning. He comes home just before I go to work."

"So you are telling me that he doesn't come home until later than he should."

"Yes, ma'am, sometimes he barely gets home in time for me to get to work. How in the world could he do that to my babies?"

"Would you like for me to talk to him?"

"No, please don't. He would get very upset, because I am letting our business out in the streets. You know how stubborn he could be."

"Yes, baby, I do. I want you to remember that you don't have to live like this."

"Yes, I know I don't, but I still love him."

"Melissa, I always want you to just remember one thing."

"What's that, Mother?"

"That love is not supposed to hurt."

"You are right."

"I will always continue to pray for you and Deon."

"Thanks, Mother. Please continue to do that for me. Mother,

can I say one thing?"

"What's that?"

"At times it is rather hard for me to pray."

"Well, why is that?"

"When I am so angry and crying, I can't think of praying. I just want to leave."

"No Melissa, you always need to keep a little prayer deep down inside of you. You never know when the enemy decides to come and take over you. Just try and keep a very close relationship with God. When I am not around, there is no one to help you but him. I can't be here all the time."

"Yes, Mother, you are right."

"I know I am. What do you think I had to do?"

"What do you mean?"

"When I was married to your father, it wasn't always good."

"That is very hard for me to believe."

"No, we both had our share of ups and downs."

"I never knew that."

"It took the both of us to know who God was. There were many times that we both wanted to walk out of our marriage. It took a lot of praying from our parents. Melissa, your dad and I were both hard-headed and stubborn. God made sure that we didn't have any children until we were both saved. At first, I didn't understand why God was doing that, but the older I got, the wiser I became. All I am telling you is that you are the opposite of your father and me. You already have all of your children. So now you and Deon have to both become saved."

"Well, Mother, if I didn't believe in God, I would say that it will be impossible for Deon to become saved."

"I am so glad that you do know how good God is."

"Yes, ma'am, I do." As my mother and I were talking, Deon entered the room. He asked us if we were ready to start the party. "Yes," I shouted, "let's get this party started!" I said to myself, "I wonder how long was Deon standing at the door listening?"

I was so grateful how Kimberly's party turned out. She was very happy with all of the toys that she had gotten. She was especially happy when she received her favorite baby doll. She named her baby Ni-Ni. I didn't know where in the world that name came from, but she seemed to love it. If my baby loves it, then I guess I have to like it. This was a very fun, but long day, and I was so glad that it came to an end.

Full of anger

Later that night, after getting the kids ready for bed, Deon came in the room and wanted to talk. I was surprised to know that he was finally ready to talk to me. So I quickly sat on the bed just to hear what he had to say.

"Melissa, I need to ask you one thing."

"Sure, Deon, what is it?"

"How much does your mother know about you and me?" His demeanor started out so calm. Then it changed so quickly.

"What are you talking about, Deon?"

"You know darn well what I am talking about. I know that you have told your mother what's been going on in our marriage."

"Hold on, Deon. Where are you getting this from?"

"Just admit it. Have you told your mother anything about us?"

"No, not really, Deon."

"So that sounds like a yes."

"Well, I haven't told her much."

"I know that you are lying, Melissa."

"Why do you think I'm lying to you?"

"Earlier I was at the door listening to you and your mother's conversation."

"Okay."

"I heard you telling her that I don't do much around the house."

"No, I didn't say that."

"Yes you did, Melissa! I can tell you exactly what you said."

"Wait! Hold on, Deon, why are you yelling at me?"

"Do you want to know why I am yelling?"

"Yes I do."

"I'm so sick and tired of your mess. You think that you are so much better than other people."

"I don't think that. I have never in my life felt that way."

"You are a liar, Melissa."

"A liar?"

"Yes, that's what I said."

"I am not a liar, Deon! I am sick and tired of trying to please you."

"So, Melissa, what are you going to do about it?"

"I am just going to pray."

"Is that all you can do?"

"No, that is all I am going to do."

"I am so sick of your mess."

"Hold on, Deon, I need you to back up."

"Do what, Melissa?"

"I said back up off of me!"

"No! I will not."

"Stop squeezing my arm! Deon, stop!"

"No, Melissa, you deserve everything that you get. The best thing for you to do is hush your mouth."

As the tears flowed from my face, Deon would not stop hurting me.

"I refuse for you to yell, while the kids are in bed. If you wake up any one of them, I will mess you up!"

"I don't understand why you are so full of anger."

"If you look in the mirror, you will understand."

"You know what? I am not going to take any more of this."

"What are you going to do, pray? I am so sick and tired of you praying. I can help you get to God much quicker. Take that." He swung and struck me across my face.

"Deon, don't put your hands on me."

Again he swung. "Take that."

"Stop slapping me. Stop!"

"No I will not. You keep telling your mother all of our business. Make sure you go and tell her that! As long as we are together,

Melissa, I will do whatever I please."

"What is that supposed to mean, Deon?" I cried out.

"Don't you worry about it. I can show you better than I can tell you."

Lord, please move him out of my way before I do something that I may regret later. Please, Lord. The more I was crying, the harder I was praying. I need you more than ever. As soon as I finished praying, Deon took his keys and left the house to go who knows where. I knew that he would be gone for a while. This was my worst day of being with my husband. I was so afraid to tell my mother, because I felt that Deon might find out.

Kimberly tells all

Two weeks later, I decided to go grocery shopping. Kimberly was the only one who wanted to go. It didn't matter because I wanted to spend a little time with her. My other four children had wanted to stay home with their father. I didn't mind, because he needed to spend as much time as he could with them. As we were walking around the store, Kimberly and I were doing a lot of talking. I asked her, "How has your day been going?"

She replied, "It was fine"

"Okay, is that all?"

That wasn't all she had to say. "No, Mama."

"Kimberly, what is wrong?"

"Well, Mama, I like it when you spend time with me at school."

"That is so sweet to hear, but you know I have to work."

"Yes I do, but…"

"But what?"

"The kids in the classroom are so rude."

"Rude like how?"

"Like the other day when you came in."

"Yes."

"A few of them acted like they were my friends."

"Okay."

"But as soon as you left, they were whispering about you and daddy."

"What are you talking about, Kimberly?"

"Please, Mama, don't say anything."

"Okay, baby, I won't."

"They were saying that Daddy was cheating on you."

"What?"

"Yes, ma'am. This girl named Tina said that my daddy was at her house the other night, with her mother. Then, this mean girl named Angela said that my father was at her house a week ago. Mama, Angela thought everything was funny because she started picking on me. I told Angela that I was going to tell my mother, but she said that she doesn't care."

"What! There is no way." I couldn't believe what I was hearing.

"I said the same thing, but Mama - ."

"Yes."

"This boy named Kelvin said that my daddy took him to the store and bought him a pair of shoes. Mama, how could he do that?"

"I don't believe those children, Kimberly!"

"I know, Mama; I didn't at first either until Kelvin said that. He promised me it was true. He even knows my phone number and he never talks to anyone. He even described my daddy's car to me. I do remember that day because Kelvin was looking at me kind of strange with his new pair of shoes. Mama, I became so angry and started to cry, but my friend John told me that everything is going to be okay."

"Oh yes it is, baby." As I turned my face, I said, "I am so upset right now; I just don't know what to do."

"Well Mama, Grandma always tells me to pray. Maybe you can pray."

"I know, baby, and I want you to know something."

"What's that?"

"You are so sweet and don't you ever forget that."

"Mother?"

"Yes, Kimberly."

"How was your day?"

"It was nice up until now. Why do you ask?"

"I was just asking, Mama. Can I ask you something else?"

"What, baby?"

"Why does Daddy yell so much?"

"What do you mean?"

"I hear him yelling at you all the time. What's wrong, Mother?"

"Oh nothing. I just think your daddy is a little tired. That's all."

"Okay Mama."

"Well, Kimberly, how have your brothers and sisters been treating you?"

"I am so glad that you asked."

"Why? What's wrong?"

"The other day, Daddy was taking a nap. All four of them had the nerve to go into Daddy's pockets. Guess they were trying to take his money."

"So what did you do?"

"I just stood behind them watching, but Mother, I didn't have anything to do with it."

"I believe you."

"Mother, do you know what happened?"

"No, Kimberly, what?"

"Ernest dropped a quarter on the floor and Daddy jumped up only to find me in the room."

"Kimberly, how in the world did you get caught?"

"Well, as soon as the money dropped, all of them ran out of the room, but me. I had gotten pushed down."

"So what happened?"

"Daddy told me to come over to him, and I did. He grabbed me by my arm and asked me what I was doing in his room and why I was messing in his pockets. I told him that I was not the only one in there. So he wanted me to go and get everyone that was in there."

"Well, did you?"

"Yes, but when I did, they told me not to tell on them."

"How in the world could they say that? Kimberly, I hope that you told on them?"

"Nope. I couldn't."

"Why not, Kimberly?"

"They told me if I tell on them, they would take my baby doll away from me and throw her into the trash. I just couldn't let that happen to her."

"My poor baby. Well, I am off for the next two days. I will make sure I will drop you off at school for those days."

"Would you really, Mother?"

"Yes, baby, I will."

"I can't wait until you don't have to work so hard. I miss you being home with me. I try to stay in my room until I know that you are coming home."

"Baby, don't worry. I will probably not be working much longer."

"Why do you say that, Mother?"

"Baby, I just feel it. As for now, just make sure you pray and ask God to keep you covered."

"I already do."

"Oh, by the way, did you get into any trouble, when you told your daddy that no one else was in the room with you?"

"Yes, I got a beating. I was so glad when he stopped, because I had marks all over my body."

Lord, please help keep my baby covered with your blood. I just don't want him to take his anger out on my baby.

In the midst of my storm

Later that night after dinner, Deon and I were in the room talking. He has been drinking, because I could smell it on his breath. He kept his alcohol hidden under our bed.

While we were talking, he began yelling very loudly at me. "Melissa, you know we can't handle all of these children."

"What, Deon? Handle what children? You are barely here to handle any of them!"

"Melissa, I have told you from the beginning that we didn't need to have Kimberly."

"Deon, get out of my face, because you are drunk! I refuse to hear you talk about my Kimberly like this."

"Drunk? So what if I have been drinking."

"Deon?"

"What do you want, Melissa?"

"What is really going on with you, because you have never been a drinker."

"Melissa, you would be a drinker, if every day you had to come home and see the same person over and over again. So when I look at you, I just don't have any other choice but to drink."

"Deon, why are you so hateful? What have I done to make you this way?"

"You never listened to me."

"What?"

"You heard me. You never listen to anything that I have to say."

"Explain yourself, Deon."

"For instance, Kimberly."

"What about Kimberly?"

"You knew I didn't want to have her. You knew that."

"Deon, please don't bring up that subject."

"Why not? Don't you want me to be honest with you?"

"Please."

"Please what, Melissa? I want you to hear me and hear me well."

"What!"

"I am sick and tired of being the husband that you want me to be. I know I may not be happy being with you, but as long as we have children together, I will be here."

"Deon, I don't want you to be here if you are not happy with this marriage. I don't want having kids together to be your excuse. If being in this marriage is not for the both of us, there is no use."

"Melissa, I can't promise you that this marriage will ever be for the both of us."

"I am tired, Deon. I have cried many nights. I just don't have the tears anymore. Lord, please help my marriage."

"There you go again, asking God for help. There is no need."

"Well, Deon, if you don't want to be with me anymore, I think it is best for you to pack your clothes and leave."

"Leave? How dare you tell me to leave my house? I will never leave anything that I pay for every month. If anyone leaves, it will be you."

"Well, maybe I just will."

"What? Melissa, what did you just say?"

"Never mind, Deon."

"I asked you, what did you say?"

"I said never mind, Deon."

"If you don't want to tell me what you just said, then I will show you."

"Stop, Deon!"

"Stop what?"

"Please stop hitting me."

"For what? You are so hard-headed, I think the only way that I can make you listen to me, is if I put my hands on you. Suck it up, Melissa! Do you think I care about those tears? I am so sick and tired of you crying."

Hours later, Deon tried to make everything better. "Sorry, Melissa, I didn't mean to push you up against the wall. I apologize."

"What? You apologize? For what, Deon? What are you apologizing for? You know what you had just done to me."

"Well maybe I did, but I guess you need to do what you are good at."

As I was crying, I asked him, "What's that?"

"Pray."

"Don't worry, Deon, I have already done that."

As I walked and reached for the door, Deon grabbed my hand and told me to dry up all of my tears from my eyes, because he didn't want the kids to see me upset. So he reached for a towel, and threw it at me. I rushed out of the room and went into the restroom, to cry and pray. While I was praying, Deon knocked on the door and asked me what I was cooking for dinner.

Lord, I ask you to give me strength in the midst of my storm.

Keeping secrets

Today was my day off. I was so happy, because I was able to get my baby Kimberly from kindergarten. She was going to be surprised to see me, because I had dropped her off this morning and I also had eaten lunch with her. So she didn't have any idea that I would be here to pick her up.

Finally, the bell rang, and there went my baby waiting in line to get on her bus. "Kimberly. Hey, baby, mother is here to pick you up."

"Mother, hey I am so glad that you are here to get me."

"Oh you are?"

"Yes I am."

As Kimberly gave me a hug, I told her not so tight. She replied, "Sorry, Mother, I didn't mean to hurt you."

"No problem, baby. I am just a little sore there."

As I was putting the seat belt around her, she asked, "Mother, are you all right?"

"Yes baby, why do you ask?"

"Your eye is black."

"It is?"

"Yes it is. Did Daddy do that to you?"

"What?"

"Just tell me the truth. Did he do that?"

"I don't know why you would think that your daddy would do something like that. I just fell down at work."

"Mother, no you didn't, because you didn't have to work today, and plus you had spent most of your day with me."

I was trapped with nowhere else to turn. "Yes, baby, he did."

"How could he do that?"

"Kimberly, this will be our little secret. Please don't tell anyone."

"Mother, I feel you should at least tell Aunt Jessica."

"No, when I say no one, I mean no one. I just don't want anyone else in our family business. It's bad enough you already know."

"I only know, because whenever you and daddy argue, I am always at the door listening."

"What!"

"Yes I am. I just don't want anything bad to happen to you."

Wow, I remembered that Deon had told me the same thing about himself when he was younger. My Kimberly was just like her father. If only he would just pay attention to her.

"Mother?"

"Yes, baby."

"When Daddy was fussing at you, I wanted so bad to go in the room and help you, but I was just too scared."

"Don't baby, please don't, because you know your daddy. He would not only hurt me, he would hurt you also."

"Yes I know."

"You are so smart for a five-year-old."

"Mother?"

"Yes Kimberly."

"I heard you and Daddy fussing one day, and I heard him tell you that he regrets having me."

"What?"

"Yes Mother, that's what I heard him say."

"Well baby, that was probably the one day that your daddy was drinking."

"No, Mother, it was not."

"How do you know he wasn't drinking that day?"

"When he came in the house, he didn't have that smell on him."

"What smell?"

"It's a very bad smell."

"I don't think he said that, but if he did, just ignore him."

"I have something else to tell you."

"Now what is it?"

"You have to promise me that you won't say anything."

"What is it, Kimberly?"

"No, Mother, do you promise?"

"Yes, Kimberly, I promise."

"One day when everyone was playing, I walked into the living room only to see Daddy on the phone. At first, I thought he was talking to you, but he wasn't."

"Okay."

"I don't know her name."

"Her!"

"Yes."

"Why do you think it was a woman?"

"Mother, I heard him tell her, 'I can't wait to come over and see you tonight.' Then he said, 'Make sure you wear that sexy lingerie that I had bought you.' Mother, what is lingerie?"

"It's nothing, baby." I was saying to myself, "You are too young to know."

I knew it; I knew he was cheating on me. That was my worst fear. Lord, I know that I must lean and depend on you, but I want to kill him. After all that we have been through. I refuse to keep living like this.

"Mother?"

"Yes, baby."

"Are you okay?"

"Yes, I am just fine."

"I love you."

"I love you too."

While a tear fell from my eye, my heart was beating nonstop, and my head was pounding. I wanted so badly to seek revenge, but I knew that wasn't Christ-like.

Later that evening, Deon was getting ready for work. I decided to cook him a delicious meal, and take it to him while he was at work. As the kids and I arrived at his job, it seemed a little strange, because his vehicle was nowhere in sight. I drove all over his job parking lot and there was no sign of his car. I was beginning to think the worst, but I wanted to give him the benefit of the doubt. So I called his office, from the front desk. Someone answered, "May I help you?"

So I asked, "May I speak to Deon please?"

"Deon is not working tonight."

"Are you sure he's not at work?"

"Yes, I am sure."

With a puzzled look on my face, I responded, "This is his wife. Would you please do me a favor and check one more time, because when he left the house, he told me that he was on his way to work."

"Mrs. Sawyers, like I had already told you, your husband is not at work."

"Okay, well do you know where he could be, because when he left home, he was dressed for work?"

"I really don't have a clue, ma'am. The last I checked, Deon is off for the next two days."

"Oh, okay thank you."

I couldn't believe this. I hoped that he was not out cheating on me. I hoped and prayed that my girl Kimberly heard her father wrong. I just knew the man that I married was no cheater! Lord, please protect him, while he's out who knows where. Please, Lord, bring my husband back home to me, and our kids safe and sound. Please remove any evil and demonic spirits from him. Please, I am praying that he is not in any accidents. I don't know how I will live without my husband. Amen.

As I was praying, tears were just flowing down my face. I began to yell, "Help me, Lord. Please, I am asking you for help." I didn't know what else to do. I just wanted to know, how in the world a person can just change like this. How? I had tried so hard to do what was right as a wife. If Deon was out there cheating on me, I felt that I needed to do what was right, which was to go to the store and purchase some condoms. I knew I couldn't trust him. Not now.

If I was wrong, I wouldn't have to use them, but for now, I was going to keep myself protected.

All of a sudden, I felt someone touch me on my shoulders. As I looked back, it was my baby Kimberly. At that point, I felt comfort.

"Mother, are you all right?" she asked.

"Yes, baby, it is just my allergies acting up."

"I understand, Mother," she whispered into my ear. "Everything will be okay."

"Yes, I know it will."

"No Mama, I promise. You just wait and see."

"Thank you, Kimberly. All we can do is pray."

"Yes, ma'am, I will."

While Kimberly and I were talking, my other babies were yelling, "Mother, can we get some ice cream?"

"Please!" Kimberly replied. "Ice cream! How could you want ice cream at a time like this? Don't you all see that Mother is sad?"

"Yes, but we still want some ice cream."

Just to shut their mouths, I decided to take them to eat some ice cream. Lord, it is only you who can bring me out of this storm.

My heart can't take anymore

The next morning, as I was getting out of my bed, I was shocked to see my baby girl Kimberly lying right beside me. I tapped her on her shoulder, just to tell her to get up, because her father should be coming home in a few. She jumped up and ran to her room. I was so glad, because she made it out just in time. Deon came home ten minutes later.

As he walked into the room to take a bath, I asked him, "How was work last night?"

He replied, "The same as usual."

"Well Deon, the kids and I came to your job to bring your dinner, but they said you weren't there."

"Who in the world told you that I wasn't there?"

"One of the employees."

"I don't know what they were talking about. Besides, who told you to come to my job?"

"No one, I just knew that you left here without your dinner."

"From now on, Melissa, before you think about coming to my job, let me know. I don't need any surprise visits."

"Deon, I have a question for you."

"What is it, Melissa?"

"Are you cheating on me?"

"What!"

"I just want to know, are you cheating on me?"

"No, I'm not. Why are you asking me that?"

"So where were you last night?"

"Don't you question me, Melissa."

"Deon, I just want to make sure that my marriage is secure."

"It is secure enough."

"I just don't know what else to do. Deon?"

"What is it, Melissa? Please don't stress me out, because I am really tired. Plus, I have been working all night. So if you are getting ready to say something that I don't want to hear, it is best for you to save it."

"Yesterday I was at the grocery store, and for some strange reason, there was a lady staring at me."

"So why are you telling me this?"

I had to really come up with a quick lie. "She came over to me and asked if I was married to Deon Sawyers. I told her, 'Yes I am.' She wanted me to know that she had been sleeping with you for the past two months and she may be pregnant"

"What! Pregnant? You know I don't have anyone pregnant! Melissa, she is a liar!'

"That's what I said, until she showed me a picture of you and her together and that's when I realized that she wasn't lying to me."

"Oh, I know who that was."

"Oh you do?"

"Yes, that was my cousin Tasha."

"Oh, Tasha?"

"Yes baby."

I knew Deon was full of it. "If she is your cousin, how come I never met her?"

"She is a long-distance cousin of mine."

"Oh okay. So if she is a long-distance cousin, why did she say that she was pregnant from you, and not only that, why did you two take the picture so close together like you were a couple?"

"She is a cousin who always likes to joke around a lot."

"I would like to meet that cousin one day, because I didn't like the way she approached me."

"That will be no problem."

"Well, Deon, I have the shower running for you."

"Thank you, baby."

"While you are taking your bath, I will go and prepare breakfast for us."

"Melissa, that sounds good, because I am starving."

I knew Deon was full of mess because he had not called me baby in a long time.

While Deon was taking his bath, I decided to check all of his pockets. As I was looking through them, I was so shocked to find a few phone numbers in there. I was so pissed off; I grabbed every one of them and tore them all up. I refused to have all of those evil spirits in my house. Now I was really getting pissed, because reality had set in. I discovered a piece of paper folded up inside his pocket. It was a pregnancy test, from a local clinic. My hands were shaking and my heart started racing. I just knew that Deon didn't have another woman pregnant. All the things he had been through as a child, I knew he was not following in his father's path of being a cheater.

I was so angry that I decided to check inside his underwear, to make sure he hadn't been out there sleeping with anyone last night. Oh my gosh! How could he! There were tiny white stains all inside of his underwear. How nasty could he be? That meant he cheated and he didn't wear a condom. Now, that's when reality had definitely set in. I had a no-good husband! How in the world could he go out in the streets and sleep around on me. I didn't deserve this. Lord, please help me to get through this. I just don't know what to do. Let me hurry up, because Deon is getting ready to get out of the shower.

I tried my best to put Deon's clothes back the way he left them, because I didn't want to hear his mouth. But it was too late. "Melissa, what are you doing!" Deon said with a harsh voice.

"Huh?" I replied.

"I asked you, what are you doing messing with my clothes?"

"Oh nothing, Deon, I was getting ready to wash a load of clothes and I just thought you would have liked for me to wash yours."

"No, you know that I don't like you to wash my clothes."

"Well, I was just trying to be nice."

"How long will it be before breakfast is ready?"

Oh my God, I said to myself, I never made it to the kitchen to start cooking. "Oh, it won't be too much longer."

"How long will that be, Melissa? I need to try and get me some rest."

Ha! I quietly said to myself. I mumbled, "I bet you do."

"What?"

"Nothing," I replied.

"No, I think I heard you say something."

"Deon, I was just talking to myself."

"Did you say, 'I bet you do'?"

"No, Deon, you were just hearing things."

"I know what I heard, Melissa. Now did you say that?"

"Yes, Deon, I did."

"What is your problem, Melissa?"

"Deon, I don't have a problem. Wait a minute, Deon, you know what? I do have one."

"Well, Melissa, what is it?"

"Deon, is there something you need to tell me?"

"No, why do you ask?"

"Well, Deon, as I was getting ready to wash your clothes, a condom fell out of your pockets, and not only that - what is this?"

"What is what?"

"This."

"Oh. Um. Yeah."

"Deon, is that all you can say? You better tell me now what's going on. To me, this looks like a pregnancy test. Am I right?"

"Yes you are."

"Okay, is that all that you can say? So do you have someone out there pregnant with your child?"

"Melissa, I don't know, because I was not the only one she was with."

"Deon, how could you do this to me after all we have been through? So now you are admitting to me that you are cheating on me?"

"Yes, but it was only one time, and I wore a condom."

"I am not done with you. Deon, what about all of those telephone numbers that were inside your pockets? Do you have an explanation?"

"No I don't."

"Well explain this." I grabbed his underwear and showed him the semen that was inside of it. Deon became extremely angry with me!

"Give me back my underwear. Better yet, keep your hands off of my clothes. I knew you weren't trying to wash my clothes. You just wanted to be nosy. I also bet that you didn't have any intention to cook. You never cook this early. Melissa, I bet you haven't cracked the first egg! Have you? That was just your excuse to get me to take my bath."

"I am not saying anything to you, Deon, because you don't have any room to fuss at me. I have been a great wife to you. As far as I am concerned, this conversation is useless!"

"Useless! What do you mean by that? Melissa, I know you are not calling me useless!"

"I didn't say that."

"Well, it sounded like that. Get over here!"

"No, I will not."

"I said, get your butt over here right now!"

"No! Deon, I won't."

"That's alright. I will just come to you."

As I was trying to run out of the bedroom, Deon grabbed me by my neck and pushed me against the wall.

"Stop Deon, I refuse to take any more of your beatings." He grabbed me tighter and dropped me down onto the floor. "What are you doing?" I jumped up off the floor and yelled, "Please, put that board down!"

"No, I am going to bust you upside your head." As I quickly ducked, Deon missed my head. "I am so sick and tired of your mess, Melissa."

"Deon, I don't know what has come over you, but I'm not going to put up with your mess any longer."

"So what are you going to do about it? You don't have anywhere else to go, and plus, you don't have any money. Oh I forgot, you can go back to your little old mother's house." Deon continued ranting, "Well, Melissa, like I told you before, I am not leaving my house. Not as long as I pay the mortgage every month."

"Deon, I am so tired of you complaining about what goes on in our house. You are not here half of the time. I may have bruises all over my body, but that's just temporary. My heart has ached long enough and my eyes have cried their last tears."

"Melissa, I know that if you leave, you will definitely be back. Just watch!"

"Deon, I can show you better than I can tell you."

"You know what, Melissa, I am running off for a few hours, and when I get back, you and my children better not be gone!"

"Ok, Deon."

Ten minutes later, Deon finally left. As soon as he was gone, I quickly grabbed all of our clothing. I knew that I already had enough of his mess. I thought the only way that he would get his mess together was by being alone. Before we left, I decided to call and tell my best friend Jessica to let her know what was going on. I knew that this would be one of the hardest things for me to do, but she would have to understand. As the phone rang, Jessica answered, "Hello."

"Hey girl, you know who this is."

"Hey Melissa. How are you? I was just thinking about you."

"I am doing fine."

"That's good, and how are my babies?"

"They are fine also." Then I got to the real reason why I was calling. "I am calling to let you know that the kids and I are moving."

"Moving," Jessica replied.

"Yes girl, there have been things going on around here, but it is just too much for me to explain."

"I understand."

"Oh you do?"

"Yes Melissa, I have been thinking about you for a while. The last time we were together, I saw some bruises all over your neck. I could also tell that your left eye was black."

"Wow Jessica, I didn't know that you knew. I always tried to hide it with makeup."

"Yes, I saw, but your makeup had rubbed off onto your shirt and that's when I saw it."

"Why didn't you say anything to me?"

"Well, Melissa, I just felt that it wasn't any of my business. If you had wanted me to know, you would have told me."

"I understand."

"I didn't want to get too involved, because you are a married woman. What goes on in your house, I feel as if you would have wanted it to stay in your house."

"Yes, I can't lie about that. That's what I told Kimberly."

"What about Kimberly?"

"She knew what had gone on between her father and me. She was very mad. She and I talked for a while about it. You won't believe it, Jessica, but Kimberly is smarter than you think."

"What?"

"She wanted me to tell you everything that's been going on, but I couldn't."

"Why?"

"I didn't want anyone to judge me or Deon."

"I can understand that."

"You know that abuse is not a part of Deon."

"Yes, I know."

"I just think the best thing for me to do is leave for now."

"So where are you all going?"

"We are going to move far away."

"Far away where?"

"We are moving to Atlanta, Georgia."

"Atlanta, Georgia! Why in the world so far?"

"I just want to move somewhere where no one knows me or my children."

"I can understand that, but North Carolina is so huge."

"No, I just want to make a change. I know it will be hard, but I can make it."

"So what does your mother have to say about it?"

"Well, I had mentioned it to her in the past, but it was just talk. I haven't told her yet."

"How do you think she will feel about it?"

"Knowing my mother, she will probably want to move with me."

"Yes, I was thinking the same thing."

"We are getting ready to leave. I have to make this last phone call to my mother, and after that, we will be on our way."

"Well, Melissa?"

"Yes, Jessica."

"I want you to drive safely and make sure you take care of your children. Call me once you get there."

"Thank you so much, Jessica, for being a real and true friend to me. I will ever be so grateful to you. I love you with all of my heart."

"Melissa, I will always support you in everything you do. That's my job."

"Thank you."

"No, thank you. Hey, Melissa, don't forget to give my babies a kiss for me."

"I will."

"Bye. See you later. May God continue to bless you."

"Thanks."

As soon as Jessica and I had finished talking, I called my mother. I knew that I didn't have much time before Deon would get back home. My mom gave me her blessings, and told me that she had already felt it in her heart that I would be leaving. She just didn't know the time or place. I was so happy that she had given me her blessings and love. I felt that leaving Deon for now would be the best thing for me to do. Lord, as I make this journey, please keep me covered in your blood.

The move

I looked around and realized that I had to send a special prayer to God:
As I sit here, wondering if I should stay or go, I know deep down in my heart that I really don't know. I am so tired of the abuse and being misused. Lord, please give me strength because I don't have a clue. Wondering each day if he really loves me with all the screaming, yelling, fighting how could it be. Lord, I really need for my man to be whole and complete. Would you please save Deon and bring him back to me?

As I packed all of our belongings and loaded up the car, I turned back for one last look and all I could remember was my scars on my face. Lord, I can't do this alone, I can't win this race. Thank you, Lord, for lending me your ear, with all of the praying that I have done; now I don't ever have to fear.

Amen.

Moving to Atlanta, Georgia was the hardest thing for the kids and I to do. Catherine, Leon, and Ernest have not been very happy. Each night, they would cry for their father. They just didn't know how hard it was for me to be without him. So I could imagine how they felt. My daughter, Nichole, had not said a word about moving. So I just hoped that she was not keeping it all on the inside. My girl Kimberly was very happy, because she didn't have to hear any fussing and yelling. I was surprised, because she never brought up the subject about us leaving her father. I thought that being around Deon, really made her fearful of him. That is so sad for a child to feel that way, especially about her own father. Lord, I ask you to keep my kids covered in your blood and please protect them from all hurt, harm, and danger.

It had been two years since the kids and I had been living in Atlanta, Georgia. I was blessed because Catherine was now in the eleventh grade, the twins were in the eighth grade, and Nichole was in the fifth grade, and my baby Kimberly was in the fourth grade. They were doing great in school. Catherine had been nominated to be the homecoming princess for her junior class in high school. I was so excited for her, but something still seems to be bothering her.

"Is there a problem, Catherine?"

"I don't know who I can get to walk with me."

"What do you mean?"

"I am just saying that the night of our homecoming game, I would need a male escort."

"Well, you could ask your Uncle Robert, if you like."

"I guess I could."

"Catherine, do you have anyone else in mind?" I said to myself, "I hope my girl doesn't have any of those boys on her mind. She knows that she can't date anyone until she graduates from high school." That might sound mean, but I remember my mother didn't let me date until I was in the eleventh grade. I had thought about giving her that opportunity to date then, but I changed my mind, because not too long after I had started dating, I had gotten pregnant. I thought the best thing for me to do was pray and let God lead me into making the right decision.

"Mother?"

"Yes."

"Are you listening to me?"

"Yes, Catherine, what did you say?"

"I said that I am praying that my father would be able to walk with me."

"Your father?"

"Yes."

"All you can do about that is pray. You know we haven't talked to him since we left. I had gotten messages that he was so sorry and he regrets all that he had done, but I still don't think he is ready to be with us."

"In my heart, Mother, I think he is."

"I hope your heart and my heart would work together. Your grandmother has been keeping in touch with your father and she told me that he is doing fine."

"That's good right?"

"Yes it is."

"So are you and my father going to get back together?"

"I don't know, baby. I have been seeking God's face."

"Mother, how long are you going to keep seeking His face? It's been over six years."

"Well, baby, it's only been two years since we've been gone."

"You may be right, but with all of the problems that you and Daddy have been having, it is really more like four."

"Yes that's true."

"Don't you think by now, Mother, it's time for you two to let bygones be bygones?"

"Maybe, but you don't understand, baby."

"I think I do, Mother."

"I hope you do, because I have been praying for your father for a very long time."

"Yes I know. If you don't mind, may I ask you another question?"

"Yes, Catherine."

"Why are you still wearing your wedding ring?"

"Well, it is not like I don't love your father."

"Wow!"

"We have a good history together. I still love him, but I just don't love his ways."

"So what are you trying to say?"

"I am saying that if your father would change his ways about himself and get saved, I will probably take him back, but I don't know if that would ever happen."

"Mother, like you have always said, just pray."

"Yes, that's the joy that God has given you: Prayer."

"I want you to know another thing, Mother."

"What?"

"Thank you for not having different men around us. I am happy that you are my mother. When I get older, I want to be just like you."

"Oh no! As for me inviting men into our house, I am a better woman than that. Plus, I don't ever want you to be like me."

"No, Mother, I really do."

"Just listen to me, Catherine. I had to go through a lot to get to where I am now. So I don't wish this on my worst enemy. Now, what I would like for you to learn from me is..."

"Is what, Mother?"

I want you to learn how to pray to God, not just when the times are rough, but also when they are going good."

"Yes, ma'am, I will."

"Not just that, I also want you to know that going to church and learning more about Jesus will help you go a long way."

"I promise. Is that why you're so strong, Mother?"

"Yes, I guess that's why. If ever you talk to your father again, he will tell you that praying was something that I had to do on a daily basis."

"Yes Mother, I must admit, you have done a lot of praying."

"Well, when you go through the things like I had to go through, baby, that's all you can do."

"Mother, I must commend you for that."

"Like I had always said, if it wasn't for the Lord on my side, it is no telling where I would be."

"You got that right! I may not act as if I didn't care when you and my father used to argue, but I did. I just didn't have the right words to say."

"I can understand that."

"I just didn't like how my father used to treat you."

"Well Catherine, I didn't either."

"Don't get me wrong, Mother, there were times when I wanted to… well when we wanted to…"

"Who is we?"

"Ernest, Leon, and I."

"What was it that you all had wanted to do?"

"Well, since our father is not here, I will tell you. One day, we were planning to take all our father's money out of his pockets."

"For what?"

"We just got tired of him leaving us. We really used to get angry when he would leave you. Growing up, we used to do some horrible things just to make sure our father wouldn't leave the house, but most of the time, things would backfire on us."

"Yes I heard."

"How did you know?"

"Most of the horrible things that you and the other three had done had gotten Kimberly in trouble."

"Yes, we just knew that our father would have beaten us like we had stolen something. I just couldn't put up with that."

"You couldn't put up with it, but what about Kimberly, who had to take all of the beating for the four of you?"

"Yes I know, the older we got, the guiltier we felt. We knew it was wrong, and just recently, we went to Kimberly and apologized to her."

"Oh you did?"

"Yes, ma'am, we all did."

"Well, I am so glad to hear that. Being your mother, I knew I didn't raise any of my children that way."

"No, ma'am, you didn't. Hey, Mother?"

"Yes."

"Is our grandmother still coming tomorrow?"

"Yes she is."

"Good, I really miss her."

"How can you miss her, when she was just here two months ago?"

"I do, because I love her so much."

"Well, she loves you too."

"Hey Mother, what's for dinner tonight?"

"Tonight is going to be an easy night, because it's the weekend."

"I think you like having an easy night, because that means you don't have to cook."

"Yes, Catherine, that's what that means."

"Okay, how about pizza?"

"Pizza sounds good to me!"

"Well pizza it is!"

The next day, I was so happy to see my mother arrive. All of the kids were jumping and yelling, "Grandma, Grandma, we love you!"

"Aw," she replied, "I love you all too."

"How long are you going to be here?" asked Kimberly

"I don't know. As long as you'll have me."

"Okay, Grandma," said Ernest, "we want you to stay forever."

"I don't know about forever, but I can stay for a long time."

"Well, that sounds good to me," said Nichole.

"Hey Mother, how have you been?"

"I have been great. The flight wasn't so bad."

"That's good to hear. How long was it?"

"It only took me about one hour to get here."

"Praise the Lord, because if you would have driven your car, there is no telling how long of a drive you would have had."

"Yes, Melissa, I know."

"I am so glad that you will be here with us for a while. I really need you here with me."

"Like I always told you, I will always be here if you need me. That's a promise."

"Well, thank you."

"Baby, you don't ever have to thank me, because that's my job."

While my mother and I were talking, the telephone began to ring. As I rushed to answer the phone, my son Leon had already answered it. "Hello," Leon said.

"Hey Auntie Jessica, how are you doing? Yes, my mother is here. Would you like to talk to her? I love you too. Mother, Auntie Jessica is on the phone for you."

I was so happy to talk to my best friend Jessica, but she and I had already talked two days ago. We made a promise that we would call each other at least twice a week. Plus it was my turn to call her. Well, I guess she just missed me that much. "Hello," I said.

"Hey Melissa, how are things going?"

"Everything is going fine here. I am excited, and my mother is here."

"That's great, Melissa. I know you are happy."

"Yes, girl, I am. I couldn't be any happier."

"Well, I was calling you, because I have some bad news."

"Bad news? Is everything okay with you?"

"Yes, I'm great, but I'm calling about your husband, Deon."

"Deon?'

"Yes."

"What's the matter?"

"I think it would be best if you would come back to Raleigh and find out for yourself."

"Well, I would at least like to know what's going on, Jessica."

"Okay, Melissa, your husband is real sick. He has been sick for a while."

"How did you find out?"

"I've been keeping in touch with him, especially since you and the kids have been gone."

"Oh you have?"

"Yes, Melissa, it is nothing like that. Deon came over to my house the same day that you and the kids left for Atlanta, Georgia."

'What was his purpose for that?"

"He was looking all over town for you all."

"Okay."

"I told him that it would be best for him to get his stuff together before trying to work on the two of you."

"Why didn't you ever tell me about this?"

"Melissa, I just didn't feel like it was the right time to."

"How do you know what's the right time, when I am the one who is married to him, not you."

"Listen, Melissa. When you left, that was the hardest thing that I had to deal with. You know we have been together since we were in elementary school. I love you with all of my heart. I would never do anything to hurt you and I refuse to let anyone else hurt my best friend. So if it was for me not to tell you about Deon, so be it. I just couldn't see you being hurt again. I love you so deeply."

"I love you too."

"Don't get me wrong, Melissa, Deon has changed a lot. I am so proud of him. I just think that you need to get down here as soon as you can, because he is in the hospital!"

"Why didn't you tell me? I am on my way. I have to book my flight and I will be there."

"Okay, see you later."

"Love you, Jessica."

"I love you too, Melissa."

I was saying to myself, "Thank God that my mother is here." As I finished talking to my mother, letting her know about Deon's situation, she gave me her blessings and told me to go and check on my husband. I asked her to make sure that she and the kids would do a special prayer tonight for their father.

Praying for Deon

Finally, I arrived at St. Medical Hospital in Raleigh, North Carolina. Prior to walking into the room, I felt the spirit of my father walking beside me. I felt that he reassured me that everything would be fine with Deon. At the moment, I felt comfort. As I walked into the room, he was lying in his bed unconscious, but the positive thing about it was that he was no longer on life support. To God be the glory. All I did was rub his head and say a prayer for him. I prayed for hours, hoping that God would strengthen his body. Deon stayed unconscious for two days straight. Those were the longest two days of my life. I continued to rub his hands and whispered into his ears, just to let him know that I loved him. All of a sudden, Deon moved. I jumped back, because that was his first movement since I had been here. I quickly called for a nurse to come into the room.

She checked his vitals and said, "Deon is progressing for the best." I was so happy. She also stated, "I've never seen a patient become as strong as Deon in just two days."

I replied, "It was nothing but God. I have prayed for him since the moment I have entered his room."

"Yes, I knew you had, because every time I entered the room, you were always praying, so I didn't want to disturb you."

"I am so sorry that I have not introduced myself to you. My name is Melissa. I am Deon's..."

"You don't have to tell me. You are Deon's wife, right?"

"Yes, I am. How did you know?"

'Well, this is not the first time he has been here."

"Oh, it's not?"

"No."

"The very first time he came here was roughly about two years ago."

I said to myself, "I wonder, was it around the time the kids and I left?"

I replied, "Two years?"

"Yes, he had gotten very sick."

"Sick? Like how?"

"We discovered that Deon had an ulcer."

"An ulcer?"

"Yes."

"Wow, I never knew."

"We heard."

"What's that supposed to mean?"

"No Melissa, not like that. Two years ago, when Deon came into the hospital, he was hurting pretty bad. We also saw that he was married, but he never brought his wife along. So I decided to ask him if he would like for me to call his wife. He replied, 'No it will be a waste of my time.' He went on and on about how he treated his family and if he could make it up, he would. If I could remember correctly, I think there was another woman with him."

"Oh there was!"

"Yes," she replied.

I thought to myself, I wonder who was with my husband. Women these days, you just can't seem to trust them.

"Hold on, Melissa. I am going to go and look at Deon's records."

"Okay." While I was waiting, I was giving Deon the evil eye. I began to get a little angry at him, because he didn't have any respect for me. How could he bring another woman to the hospital with him? I was his wife! As the nurse entered the room, she showed me Deon's medical records from two years ago.

Then she asked me if I knew a person by the name of Jessica. "Jessica," I replied. "Yes I do. I have a good friend by the name of Jessica."

"Well, she was the one who brought Deon here two years ago."

"Oh! Well I am shocked because she had never told me one thing about Deon, being in the hospital."

"I don't know what to tell you, because she seemed to be a very special friend to him."

"Special! Special like how?"

"No, not like that. I took it as if she could have been a sister to him."

"Oh, a sister, yes, she is a special person." Whew that was close. I was beginning to think that my best friend was sleeping with my husband. I would definitely keep those thoughts to myself. I didn't want her to get mad at me.

While the nurse and I were talking, Deon began to open his eyes. He looked up at me as if he had seen a ghost. "Melissa," Deon said, "is that you?"

"Yes, Deon, it is me."

While he was in pain, Deon was trying to reach for my hand. "Come here, Melissa, please." Deon started to cough over and over again.

"Please, Deon, be careful." At first, I hesitated, because I didn't exactly know what was wrong with Deon. I asked, "Deon, are you okay?"

"Yes, Melissa, I should be. I think I need to tell you something."

"Yes, Deon, what is it?"

"Melissa, I have been sick for a while. I am so glad that you are here with me."

"I am glad that I am here also."

"Melissa, I have been doing a lot of thinking."

"Well, Deon, we will have time to talk later. For now, you just need to relax and try and get better."

"I am much better now."

"How could you say that? When you are lying in your bed doing a lot of coughing?"

"Melissa, I need for you to take my hand." As I grabbed for Deon's hand, I was shocked to see that he was still wearing his wedding ring. "Wow," Deon said.

"What, Deon?"

"You still have on your wedding ring."

"Why shouldn't I?"

"I just figured when you packed up all of your belongings and left, I thought you didn't want me any longer."

"What made you think that?"

"You know why, Melissa."

"No, Deon, why don't you tell me why?"

"You know I was really a butt hole to you."

"I am not going to lie. You sure were!"

"Not only to you, but I was also one to our children. The moment that you and the kids had left me, I knew that my life was going to change. I tried my best to look for you and my babies, but it was no way that I could find you all. I went to your mother's house and also to Jessica's. Neither of them would tell me where you were."

"So how did you and Jessica stay in touch?" I thought to myself, Hmm, I wonder if he and Jessica had an affair. "Well, the next day, I went back to Jessica's house to see if she would just let me know anything about you and the kids, but she was stern on her words. Then I asked her where she was heading and she told me that she was on her way to church." I thought to myself, he probably wanted to run in the other direction. Deon kept going with the story, "She asked me if I would like to go. I can't lie, Melissa. At first I hesitated, because church was the furthest thing from my mind. I just wanted to find my family, but all of a sudden, your voice came into my head."

"What was it saying?"

"Seek ye first the kingdom of God. Then you will find your answer."

"So did you?"

"Yes, from that moment on, I have been deeply involved with the church. Not only that, I have been going to a therapist. I knew I needed help."

"Wow, Deon that's great."

"Melissa, I owe it all to you. I don't want to stand here and take any of the credit."

"It wasn't me at all. All the credit goes to God. I am so happy, Deon, that you have made a change in your life."

"I am too. Melissa, I don't know why I was that evil man. I asked myself over and over again and I just couldn't seem to get an answer. With the help of my therapist, I realized that all of my issues had come from my childhood. I didn't know what or how I was going to be able to change my situation. Until, that one special day, I had turned my life over to God."

"What!"

"Yes, I am saved. I have been saved now for the past year and a half. I must admit all of the praying you had done for me, it was not in vain. I have changed for the better."

"I am happy to hear your testimony, Deon. I will be here for another day or two just to make sure you get settled at your house. I feel I could at least do that for you."

"Melissa, what in the world would I do without you?"

"I ask myself the same thing."

"You are still that comedian, Melissa. That's why I still love you."

"You what?"

"Yes, I said it right. I LOVE YOU! I haven't stopped loving you. Melissa, is it okay if I ask you something?"

"Well, Deon before you ask me anything, I have something to ask you."

"Yes."

"So how is your new baby?"

"What baby? Melissa, I don't have a baby."

"So you are telling me that she was not pregnant?"

"No, that is not what I am saying."

"So what is it?"

"All I am saying is that she was pregnant, but it wasn't my child."

As I took a deep breath and gave Deon a smile, I replied, "Yes,

Deon, you can ask me anything."

"I want to know if you would accept my apology for not being the man that God had me to be."

"Deon, I am a Christian and I would be less than a person if I don't forgive you. So yes, I will forgive you."

"Thank you so much. That was huge, Melissa. I just didn't think this moment would have ever come. Well, I do have something else to ask you."

"I am listening."

"I think I am less than a man if I bring this up to you."

"Yes, Deon, you can ask me anything."

"Okay, Melissa, what do you think about you and I getting back together again?"

"Now Deon, that's big. I can't answer that right now."

"Why not?"

"Have you thought about what you put me through and our daughter, Kimberly?"

"Yes I have, Melissa. Once I went to God, I repented. I didn't know how wrong I was until I was saved. I was very awful and stupid."

"Well, I am glad that you realized that you were wrong. Deon, Kimberly knew that you didn't want her."

"How did she know?"

"She was listening at our bedroom door when you were yelling at me."

"Oh, are you serious?"

"Yes I am. She was hurting very bad. She was at the point, Deon, where she was beginning to hate you."

"I can understand that. I didn't show her or any of you the love that I should have."

"Yes, instead of you showing us love, you showed the streets."

"Yes, you are right. I can't argue with you. I had done things that I am ashamed of. I am not worthy of you, Melissa, but I am praying to God that you will have a change of heart."

"If you don't mind, Deon, I just need to step out of the room for a moment."

"Sure, Melissa, I understand."

"I will be back in a few."

"No problem, I will be right here."

As Deon began to giggle, I asked him, "Now who's being the comedian?"

"I guess I am."

"You guessed right."

While I was walking down the hall, I had memories of my father lying in that hospital bed. I was so blessed that Deon was still alive. I just needed to get some air, just so I could think.

As I was walking, I stopped to get a sip of water. At that moment, a doctor approached me. "Hi, are you Melissa Sawyers?"

I nodded my head and stated, "And may I ask, who are you?"

"Hi I am so sorry, my name is Dr. Gardner, and I am your husband's doctor. I wanted to introduce myself sooner, but each time I would check in on Deon, you were deep in prayer or just stepped out of the room."

"Oh, how did you know that Deon is my husband?"

"He has been coming to me for the last two years."

"Okay"

"He also showed me a few pictures of you and the children."

"He has?"

"Yes."

"So what is really going on with Deon?"

"Well, Deon has had a lot of problems."

"Oh."

"Yes, the first visit he had with me, he was sick and depressed."

"When you say 'sick', what do you mean by that?"

"No, not like a disease sickness. Deon has been sick for the past two years. He had been under so much stress, which caused him to have an ulcer."

"I wonder what kind of stress he had been under."

"Well, Melissa, I am not a therapist, but I have listened to Deon's problems. Most of his sickness has come from missing you and his children. He wanted me to know that his past was not the way that God had wanted him to go, but he decided to do what he felt was right. It took him getting sick to know that he was going down the wrong pathway. I was surprised that Deon trusted me the way that he did. I am so glad that he made a change when he did."

"Yes, I am too."

"Melissa, your husband really regrets everything that he did to you and the kids. I don't want to get too involved into you and Deon's marriage, but just seeing the changes that he has made over the years, it's truly a blessing."

"I am so happy that Deon has chosen you as his doctor, because just by standing here talking to you, I can tell that you really love the Lord."

"Yes, Melissa, I can admit that. He comes first in my life, before anything else."

"That's great!"

"I just wanted you to know about your husband and how special he is."

"I thank you so much, Dr. Gardner. I really needed that."

"Yes, I knew you did, and one more thing, Melissa."

"Yes sir."

"Don't forget that your husband talks about you all the time."

"I won't forget that." I wondered if Dr. Gardner was trying to get Deon and I back together again. Hmm. "Thanks a lot, Dr. Gardner, for the information."

"You are welcome."

"Oh yeah, by the way, Dr. Gardner?"

"Yes ,Melissa."

"I have one more thing to ask you."

"Sure."

"How is Deon's condition?"

"As long as he keeps his stress under control, he will be much better."

"So how did he end up back here again?"

"Deon's ulcer is very bad. Melissa, this time, his ulcer has gotten so severe, that he fell out and hit his head on his marble living room table."

"Ouch!"

"I know that God has a lot to do with Deon still living, because he should have been dead a long time ago."

"Dead! Are you serious?"

"Yes I am. It is truly a blessing that he is still alive."

Wow, now I really needed to do a lot of thinking. I really couldn't lose him. I decided to go into the hospital chapel. I just needed some one-on-one time with God. As I was praying, I heard someone enter the room. It was my friend Jessica. "Hey Jessica, how are you?"

"I am great," Jessica replied. "I decided to stop by and check on you and Deon, before going to work."

"I am so happy to see you. I have heard a lot about what you did."

"Me? You have?"

"Yes, Jessica, I have."

"I hope it was all good stuff."

"Yes it was. I just want to thank you for watching Deon while the kids and I were gone. You have been a very special friend. I just want to say again thank you."

"No problem, Melissa, I just felt that it was my job to make sure everything was okay."

"You did a great job."

"Melissa, I do have something to tell you."

"Yes, Jessica."

"While you were gone..."

"Yes."

"Deon and I have been deeply involved."

"What! Deeply involved like how?"

"No! Not like that. Heck no. We have been going to church every Sunday."

"Hey Jessica, since you and Deon have been doing a lot of talking, do you think he has made a change with his life?"

"Do I? Yes he has. He is nothing like the Deon that you had left. He is now the man that you had originally married. I can tell you one thing. Deon doesn't have time for those women out there in the streets anymore. He works morning, noon, and night. He said it is best for him to work every day except for Sundays."

"Are you serious?"

"Girl, yes, I am more than serious. Your husband has changed tremendously. It's truly a blessing."

"Oh Jessica, yes it is. I am so confused."

"Why is that, Melissa?"

"Deon had asked for us to get back together."

"Yes, I know."

"How did you know?"

"We talked about it before."

"So Jessica, what do you think I should do?"

"Melissa, you really need to follow your heart. You need to make sure that you make the right decision, but make sure that you seek God's face. He will have all of your answers."

"Thanks, Jessica, I will."

"I must be going now; I have to get to work. I will try and meet up with you and Deon tomorrow."

"Okay, I love you, Jessica."

"I love you too, Melissa. Hey Melissa, don't forget to seek God's face on your marriage."

"Yes Jessica, I will."

"Bye, for now."

As Jessica left the room, I decided to stay inside the chapel just a little while longer. I needed confirmation from God on what I needed to do with my life. I knew that I couldn't make this decision alone, so I decided to call my children, just to see how they felt about the situation. All but one was extremely happy for their father and me to get back together.

I guess it takes no rocket scientist to know which one didn't act happy. Kimberly didn't seem mad, but at the same time, she wasn't happy. I knew that I needed a one-on-one talk with my baby. "Hi Kimberly."

"Hi Mother, how are you doing?"

"I am doing fine. I guess you have heard the news about your father."

"Yes I have."

"How do you feel about your father and me getting back together again?"

"No Mother, it's not how I feel, it's how you feel. Do you think you can handle it again?"

"No Kimberly, it's not like that. Your daddy has made a huge change. He is saved."

"Did you say saved?"

"Yes, baby, your daddy is saved now. He has been going to church on a regular basis."

"Wow, Mother, that's great. I can't get mad about that."

"I know, baby. Just think about the times when you and I have prayed for your father. I really feel, deep in my heart, that he has changed."

"Well Mother, that's all I needed to hear. If you feel okay about my father, I am okay. I just want you to be happy."

"Yes, baby, I know. I have to go for now, just don't forget..."

"Don't tell me. You are going to tell me not to forget to pray."

"Yes I was. I love you."

"I love you too, Mother. See you later."

Mended pieces

I knew I had been gone for a very long time, but I wanted to make sure that all of my answers came from God. As I entered the room, Deon looked at me and said, "Melissa, I am so glad that you are back. I really missed you bad."

"I had to do a lot of thinking, about what you and I had talked about."

"I can understand that."

"Before I give you my answer, Deon, I don't think it would be fair for you to not talk to the kids. Their opinions really count."

"I know they do and I have a confession."

"What?"

"I have been talking to our children for almost the past two years."

"What!"

"Yes, Melissa, I have. Whenever Jessica and I are together and we know that you are at work, that's when we will call. I never knew the house number, but Jessica would dial it. I must confess that Kimberly and I have been talking for a while now. I had to apologize to her for everything that I had done to her. It took her some time, but she did accept it. That was a huge burden lifted off of me. I just couldn't live without you and my babies. I felt that as long as I could hear their voices, I knew everything was okay. Not only that, Melissa, you remember on Christmas and the children birthdays?"

"Yes."

"Okay, well the presents that came in the mail were not from Jessica."

"What do you mean, Deon? They had her name on them."

"To be honest, they were from me."

"What?"

"Yes, Melissa, I went shopping and asked Jessica to mail them off for me."

"Wow Deon, I figured you had forgotten about us."

"No never, I truly love my family."

"Deon, I don't know what to say. I don't know if I want to be angry or grateful."

"Please don't be angry with Jessica. She was only doing what she felt was best for me and the kids. I am ever so grateful to her for that."

"I guess you are."

"I feel like I have been betrayed, by my best friend."

"Betrayed like how, Melissa?"

"Common sense, Deon, you and I haven't talked for a very long time, and I feel if Jessica felt that it was in your best interest for you to communicate with our children, she should have at least spoken to me first!"

"I knew that you didn't want to have anything to do with me, so I had to go through Jessica. At first, she didn't want to do it, but as I became sick, she knew that it was the right thing to do."

"Yes, I guess you do have a point."

"Well, I have to say that God is good!"

"Yes, that's right, Deon. God is good."

"Melissa, have you thought about what I had asked you?"

"Yes, I have. Please, Deon, don't get me wrong. I am still in love with you. I have totally forgiven you, for all of the mental and physical abuse that you have caused me."

"Thank you, because I made a promise to God and to myself that I would never, and I mean never, put my hands on my beautiful wife again. Melissa, there have been many nights when I lay in my bed and cried. I had to really get my life focused on God. I knew my mother had never raised me that way. I just snapped!"

"I know, and there were times, Deon, when I didn't know how to approach you. It had gotten so bad that I didn't know if you were having a good day."

"I think I was just under so much stress from working so many hours, and I just lost focus on what was the best thing for me. I never knew how good I had it, until the next day after you had left."

"Why did it take you until the next day to realize it?"

"I figured that you and my babies were coming back home, but when I had talked to your mother, then to Jessica, I knew that you were gone for good. Melissa, with you being here with me right now, it's more than a blessing. Do you know what all of this means?"

"What, Deon?"

"With all of the praying that you had been doing for our marriage, it has worked."

"Yes, Deon, I must admit, God is real."

"Melissa, look at you. You are very beautiful."

"Stop it, Deon."

"No, I am serious. I can't stop looking at my beautiful wife. I want you to know that you have made me the way I am. I don't think I would have turned out this way if you hadn't left. I am so much better now than the person that you had left. I am so much older and wiser now. I would be a fool to mess up something so good. You are the air that I breathe and the water that I drink."

"Stop, Deon. You are going to make me cry. You are a mess."

"I just want you to know that I have changed."

"I know you have, but I am just confused right now."

"Okay Melissa, I understand. Before you leave, will you please let me know?"

"Yes, Deon, I will do my best."

"That's all I ask."

"Deon, whatever the decision will be, it will be from God."

"I know it will."

"Deon?"

"Yes, baby."

"Wow, Deon, you said baby. I haven't heard that word in a while."

"I have more where that came from."

"No Deon, this is serious."

"Sorry, Melissa."

"If it's the Lord's will for you and me to get back together again, then I would like for you to know one thing."

"Yes."

"The kids and I are not going to move back to Raleigh. I refuse to. They are doing so well in school."

"I can understand that."

"There are too many bad memories here for me. I just want my life to be fully anchored in God."

"Melissa, I also need that for me."

"Well, I am leaving tomorrow evening."

"Tomorrow! Why so soon?"

"I have to get back with the kids. Plus, you are doing so much better now. Deon, how about in two weeks, if you still feel the same way about us, then you can come to Atlanta, and see how you like it."

"Wait a minute, Melissa, did you say two weeks?"

"Yes, Deon. Is there something wrong with that?"

"Why not now?"

"Now?"

"Yes now."

"Deon, there is no way that you can come now."

"Why not?"

"Um, because Deon, you are in the hospital."

"Yes, Melissa, I am, but while you were gone, Doctor Gardner came in and said I will be discharged tomorrow."

"Oh he did?"

"Yes, and Melissa, guess what?"

"What, Deon?"

"He said that he can transfer my medical records to a doctor in Atlanta and I can do my follow up visit there."

"That's great!"

"Yes, that's what I said. So Melissa, if you don't mind, I want to go back to Atlanta tomorrow with my family."

"Hold on, Deon. Don't you have to get the approval from your job?"

"Yes, I have already done that."

"You did what?"

"While you were out, I transferred my job to Atlanta. I am serious, Melissa. I refuse to let my family leave me again." As Deon was talking, tears were flowing from his eyes. "I will show you better than I can tell you."

"Okay Deon, I know that this is not me talking, because I would have wanted us to wait just a little while longer."

"Well, I thank God that it's not you; I have waited well over two years."

"Yes Deon, you are so right!"

"But Melissa, I can tell you one thing for sure."

"What's that, Deon?"

"God works in mysterious ways."

"Oh, yes he does."

"Thank you so much, Melissa. I promise that you and the kids would not ever regret this."

"I hope not."

"Baby, I have indeed learned my lessons."

"Deon, if I have a God that's forgiving, why can't I be the same."

"Hallelujah!"

The next day, after Deon had gotten discharged from the hospital, we went straight to his house so he could pack all of his belongings. It didn't take him any more than one hour to get everything that he needed. I was very surprised just to see how much Deon really meant what he had said.

"Melissa?"

"Yes, Deon?"

"I have something to say."

"Yes what is it?"

"I didn't know how good God was until I found out for myself. I can remember the times we used to argue."

"No let's correct that, Deon: when you used to argue with me!"

"Okay, you are right. I could recall through all of my mess that you still prayed for me. Melissa, you stood by my side regardless of my wrongdoings. I love you so much for not giving up on me. With all the bitterness and hatefulness I had towards you, I don't deserve to be here right now, but by the grace of God, He had made a way for me to clean myself up, and my baby was still waiting on me. Melissa, I am so sorry."

"Deon, please don't cry on me."

"I can't help it, Melissa. I don't deserve you. I am not worthy of you."

"Stop, Deon. Please stop it now!"

"If it was not for the Lord on our side, I wouldn't be here."

"I know, Deon, but please hurry and let's go, because this house just gives me the creeps."

"Okay, Melissa, I really need to go to the restroom. I will be right back."

"Okay I will go and load up the car."

"Thank you so much."

While I was gathering all of Deon's belongings, I overheard him in the bathroom talking. I was so shocked because I never heard my husband pray and cry out to God. I knew that God was awesome, and if He could change someone like Deon, then He definitely could change anyone.

As the door opened, Deon happily said, "Okay Melissa, I am ready to go. I am just going to lock up the house and give my mother a key so she could check on the house from time to time."

"Sure Deon, no problem."

Finally, after 20 minutes, we made it to the airport. We just barely made it in time for our flight. Deon had treated me like I was his girlfriend all over again. I had forgotten how that felt. I sure missed that feeling!

As we arrived at the house, the children were waiting at the door for their father and me. Every one of them was yelling so loudly that I knew I made the right decision. I was so surprised just to see how Kimberly and her father embraced each other. He didn't want to let her go. I stood there crying, because I knew that having my baby Kimberly wasn't a sin. I was so happy to see the bond that she had been longing for from her father.

My mother was so happy, because she knew that Deon and I were meant for each other. She tapped me on my shoulder and said, "Melissa, don't forget even if times seem to be going good, always make sure that you continue to pray. Always remember that God is always in control."

"I love you so much, Mother."

"Melissa, you know that your mother will always love you."

"Yes, I know!"

It didn't take Catherine any time to ask her father to be her escort. A tear fell from his eye as he answered, "Baby, I wouldn't have it any other way."

The next day was Bible study. I asked Deon if he would like to stay home with the kids while my mother and I went. Deon replied, "No I will not. The kids and I are going to get dressed and we will go to Bible study as a family." While my mother was sitting in the corner with her Bible in her hand, she had a very huge smile on her face. "Anything else, Melissa, that is church-related, I want to make sure that my family and I are involved."

"We sure will. That won't be a problem."

A week later, Deon started his new job, and they were in need of someone to work a day-shift position. Deon made sure he accepted it, because he refused to let another night shift ruin our marriage.

Each week that Deon would get paid, he would hand over his paycheck. He just wanted to prove that he had really made a change. Through all of my pain and difficulties, I was happy to know that I was able to love Deon again. The more I began to trust Deon, the more I was able to tell him about the three hundred thousand dollars that I had inside my savings account.

He wasn't upset at all. He just smiled and said, "Melissa, as it is written in John 15:9 as the Father hath loved me, so have I loved you."

"Wow Deon, you are so right."

"I love you, Melissa."

"I love you too, Deon."

By the grace of God, I knew that my marriage had been saved! The best part was that we were able to mend the pieces.

Amen!